PENGUIN BOOKS
LOVE AMONG THE BOOKSHELVES

Ruskin Bond's first novel, *The Room on the Roof*, written when he was seventeen, received the John Llewellyn Rhys Memorial Prize in 1957. Since then he has published a number of novellas, short story collections, books of essays and articles, poems and children's books. He received the Sahitya Akademi Award in 1992, the Padma Shri in 1999 and the Padma Bhushan in 2014.

Ruskin Bond was born in Kasauli, and grew up in Jamnagar, Dehradun, Delhi and Simla. As a young man, he spent four years in the Channel Islands and London. He returned to India in 1955. He currently resides in Landour, Mussoorie, with his adopted family.

Love among the Bookshelves

RUSKIN BOND

PENGUIN BOOKS

An imprint of Penguin Random House

PENGUIN BOOKS

USA | Canada | UK | Ireland | Australia
New Zealand | India | South Africa | China | Singapore

Penguin Books is part of the Penguin Random House group of companies
whose addresses can be found at global.penguinrandomhouse.com

Published by Penguin Random House India Pvt. Ltd
4th Floor, Capital Tower 1, MG Road,
Gurugram 122 002, Haryana, India

Penguin
Random House
India

First published in Viking by Penguin Books India 2014
Published in Penguin Books by Penguin Random House India 2017

10 9 8 7 6 5 4 3 2

ISBN 9780143424048

Typeset in Adobe Garamond Pro by R. Ajith Kumar, New Delhi
Printed at Repro India Limited

www.penguin.co.in

MIX
Paper from
responsible sources
FSC® C047271

This is a legitimate digitally printed version of the book and therefore might not
have certain extra finishing on the cover.

Contents

Introduction   vii

1 That Week in the Jungle   1

    P.G. Wodehouse (*Love among the Chickens*)   11

2 Holiday Reading: Classics and Comics   35

    H.E. Bates   47

3 Schooldays, Rule Days   71

    W. Somerset Maugham   83

Contents

4 That Year in Jersey   111

   Charles Dickens   127

5 Those Two Years in London   139

   Richard Jefferies   157

Favourite Books by Favourite Authors   181

Introduction

Just in case the casual reader is expecting this to be the story of a torrid love affair with a librarian, I will discourage him or her from reading further by confessing that I have never made love behind a bookshelf, with a librarian or anyone else. Tall bookshelves do afford a certain amount of privacy, but so do privet hedges and disused cupboards— probably more than hotel rooms, so many of them now rigged up with surveillance cameras.

I hereby confess that I am in love with books, and bookshelves are good places to keep them, if not hide them.

This little book is about the books I read and loved when I was a boy and a young man. Books that gave me enjoyment; books that banished loneliness or depression; books that inspired me to become a writer.

You, gentle reader, will probably have loved a different set of books and authors. Well, there are hundreds of thousands to choose from, so it should be quite easy to find a number of authors who will suit your own tastes and reading preferences.

I have written this memoir as a tribute of sorts to some of my favourite authors. Naturally enough, these are writers whose books were already classics or who came to prominence in the mid-twentieth century, and the years when I was growing up and reading everything that came my way.

I have enjoyed a fairly long life, and in my time I must have read close to ten thousand books. Many were forgettable, and have been forgotten. I have also written a few—some forgettable!

Now as I enter my eighties, I still read when the light is good and my easy chair well cushioned. My eyesight is not what it used to be, and sometimes the print dances before my eyes, and occasionally funny things happen . . .

Yesterday evening, as the sitting room grew dark, I was talking to Rakesh who stood in a far corner of the room. After several minutes of chatter from me, I realized that he was not responding; so I got up and approached him, only to find that he wasn't there: I'd been talking to a Christmas tree that had been brought in by the children!

Never mind . . .

Trees are good listeners.

Ruskin Bond
December 2013

1

That Week in the Jungle

It wasn't a bookshop, or a library, or a great-aunt's hoard of romantic novels that made me a reader; it was the week I spent in a forest rest house, in what is now the Rajaji sanctuary, between Hardwar and Dehradun.

I was eight at the time, it was the winter of 1944–45, and it wasn't a sanctuary then. Everyone with a gun fancied himself a great shikari, and the jungle resounded with the sound of gunfire as tigers keeled over and deer of all kinds bit the dust. My stepfather was a keen shikari, and my mother had also accounted for a couple of big cats—one would think that an eight-year-old boy would be thrilled at the prospect of accompanying a shikar party on a safari, but I had to be forced into going.

I disliked guns; I was afraid of them, I don't know why—some ancestral memory, perhaps. And I did not derive any pleasure from watching an animal twitching on the ground as it bled to death.

On that first day in the jungle I'd been persuaded to sit on an elephant—one of the two or three that took us deep into the forest. A chital—a spotted deer—strayed into our path, and the man beside me immediately raised his rifle and fired. The chital took some time to die. Two or three more shots were fired before it finally lay still. But its struggles had unnerved the elephant (elephants are sensitive creatures), and it turned and ran from the spot, crashing through small trees and shrubs. The branch of a tree caught me across the face and nearly swept me off the elephant. Fortunately, the mahout got it under control, and apart from a few scratches I was none the worse for the experience.

But I hadn't enjoyed it. Shooting animals for sport did not make much sense to me. For one thing, they couldn't shoot back. The man who shot the defenceless chital did at least deserve to have an antler up his behind.

Next day, I declined an invitation to another excursion into the jungle. I was left in charge of the khansama while the hunting party went off in search of more victims.

I had the rest house to myself. And while exploring it, I discovered a wall cupboard with a couple of shelves full of books. Up till then I had read just a handful of books—R.M. Ballantyne's *The Coral Island*, a school reader, a poetry reader, Lamb's *Tales from Shakespeare*, retold, abridged versions of *Robinson Crusoe* and *Gulliver's Travels*, and of course my father's stamp catalogues, which had been his favourite reading. They did at least give me a penchant for geography. But this was the first time I was discovering books for myself.

How did they get there? They weren't new books. They'd been there for some time, according to the khansama. Some forest officer's secret hoard, perhaps. Or maybe there was a time when shikaris too read books.

None of them were about shikar or even wildlife or forestry.

The first one that I took from the shelf was P.G. Wodehouse's *Love among the Chickens*. And it has nothing to do with hunting wild fowl. It was a romantic comedy about chicken farming, and it featured the incorrigible Stanley Featherstonehaugh Ukridge, who was to become one of Wodehouse's most popular characters—an optimistic entrepreneur who never allowed any of his commercial disasters to keep him down. I think I learnt something from Ukridge—resilience! Anyway, I read the book in a day, pausing only to partake of the khansama's dal-and-rice lunch and pakoras for tea.

In the evening the shikaris returned looking tired and out of sorts. Apart from a couple of partridges, they hadn't shot anything. I said nothing, but inwardly I gave three cheers. There was a lot of grumbling about poachers and villagers decimating the wildlife, quite forgetting that they were the biggest culprits in this regard—often going out at night in jeeps equipped with powerful lights, turning the lights on confused and blinded animals, and then shooting them without any difficulty. Not many 'brave' hunters went into the jungle on foot; it was the jeep or the elephant for everyone from VIP to poacher.

Off they went again, and I was happy to be left behind, free to explore the bookshelf and its literary treasures.

The second of my discoveries was M.R. James's *Ghost Stories of an Antiquary*, a set of stories by a master of the supernatural. These tales were really aimed at adult readers with some sort of academic background (as most of them were set in English colleges or universities), but I had no difficulty in reading and enjoying them. They turned me into an aficionado of the ghost story, and over the years I was to indulge in the works of Algernon

Blackwood, Edgar Allan Poe, Sheridan Le Fanu, E.F. Benson and others who specialized in the genre—and then go on to write ghost stories myself.

Fortunately, I did not see any ghosts in the rest house, although the old khansama insisted that on certain days, as dusk fell, one could hear the groans of a famous shikari as he was being savaged by a man-eating tiger. 'Served him right,' was my unfeeling comment, as I returned to M.R. James and the haunted corridors of an old English castle. Ghosts were really British inventions. In India, we had *pret*s and *churel*s, who were not the same but probably scarier . . .

The shikar party continued for another three days, at the end of which several cheetahs and sambars had been shot, as well as a hyena and a jackal, but no tigers were shot or even seen.

During this time, I devoured my first Agatha Christie (*Peril at End House*), Jack London's *White Fang*, Conrad's *Typhoon* (which held me enthralled), and a book on gardening—*Down the Garden Path* by Beverley Nichols. This last stimulated my interest in gardening as a hobby, and when we returned to Dehra, I made an attempt at growing various decorative plants—with limited success, as I usually forgot to water them.

In the fast-fading evening light I was sitting on the veranda, reading, when a large animal crossed the clearing in front of me. Before I could get up, it had disappeared into the forest. The old khansama had seen it too.

'Was it a tiger?' I asked excitedly. 'It was very big.'

'Not a tiger, baba. A leopard. The leopard is the more silent of the two.'

When the shikaris returned, empty-handed this time, I mentioned that I had seen a leopard. They found this terribly amusing.

'The boy has imagination,' observed Major Kohli, a family friend. 'Here we are, beating the jungle for tigers and leopards, and he sees one while sitting on the veranda!'

'Not active enough,' said my stepfather. 'Should get out more often—join the party.'

In time I was to learn that it's the onlooker who sees more of the party than the partygoer; that it's the man on traffic duty who sees more of the passing show than the man behind the wheel; that the man on the hilltop sees the curvature of the earth better than the man on the plain; that the hovering vultures know who's winning the battle long before the opposing armies; and that, when all the wars are done, a butterfly will still be beautiful.

I did not know all this at the time, but I was learning.

'He reads too much,' said Uncle Harry. And of course he was right. I just couldn't get enough to read.

P.G. Wodehouse

(*Love among the Chickens*)

Love among the Chickens was one of Wodehouse's earliest novels. It was first published in 1906, when he was twenty-five. Twenty years later, finding it had dated a little, he brought out a revised edition and it is from this 1926 edition that the following extract is taken.

Stanley Featherstonehaugh (pronounced Fanshawe) Ukridge was one of Wodehouse's most delightful creations—a genial, happy-go-lucky scamster who came up with the wildest schemes for making a fortune, always with the most disastrous results; but his optimism never wavered, his joie de vivre could not be suppressed.

You can read more about Ukridge in the ten short stories that make up the collection called

Ukridge, first published in 1924 and still one of Wodehouse's most popular books. It tells of the time when Ukridge sets up an insurance syndicate with his friends, the success of which depends on one of them breaking a leg. His attempts at managing a boxer named Battling Billson, who has a tendency to lie down on the first round, form the bedrock of three of the most hilarious stories, along with another favourite of mine, 'Ukridge's Dog College'.

Amongst Wodehouse's great comic creations, there are other rivals for my affections—Jeeves and Bertie Wooster, probably his most popular characters; Lord Emsworth, the benign owner of Blandings Castle, where prize pigs get stolen and young men fall in love with damsels in distress; Mr Mulliner, who is always ready to tell a story over a pint of beer; and the fatuous members of the Drones Club—Bingo Little, Pongo Twistleton, et al.

P.G. Wodehouse had a long innings. He began writing in Queen Victoria's reign, and continued to do so through the reigns of Edward VII, George V, George VI and Queen Elizabeth II. He spent almost half his life in America, but his novels and stories are firmly set in an England that appears to have been untouched by War or Socialism. All is sunshine and happiness in a never-never land of amiable earls, eccentric aunts and supercilious butlers. And we wouldn't have it otherwise. When I wanted realism I turned to Graham Greene and Somerset Maugham. When I wanted romance, I turned to R.L. Stevenson and Daphne du Maurier. When I wanted mystery, I turned to Agatha Christie, Rex Stout, and dozens of clever crime writers. But when I wanted escape—from the routine of boarding-school life, or the conflicts at home—I turned to Wodehouse.

Quarrelling parents, disapproving relatives, censorious schoolmates, all faded into the distance once I was immersed in *Leave it to Psmith*, *The Inimitable Jeeves*, *Meet Mr Mulliner* or *The Crime Wave at Blandings*.

When Wodehouse died at the age of ninety-three, he had produced around a hundred novels, and I must have read at least two-thirds of his output. His plots and characters might have been repetitive, but it was language—his command of the English language and all its nuances and flexibility—that was his real strength. Never a dull sentence. The world of his creation is conjured up in a few lines:

The village of Market Blandings is one of those sleepy hamlets which modern progress has failed to touch, except by the addition of a railway station and a room over the grocer's shop where moving-pictures are on view on Tuesdays and Fridays. The church is Norman, and the intelligence of the majority of the natives Palaeozoic. To alight at Market Blandings Station in the dusk of a rather chilly spring day, when the south-west wind has shifted to due east, is to be smitten with the feeling that one is at the edge of the world with no friends near.

(*Something Fresh*, 1915, the first of the Blandings Castle saga)

And so we read on . . .

From *Love among the Chickens* (1926)

by P. G. Wodehouse

Chapter II

Mr and Mrs S.F. Ukridge

I have often thought that *Who's Who*, though a
bulky and well-meaning volume, omits too many
of England's greatest men. It is not comprehensive
enough. I am in it, nestling among the Gs:

'Garnet, Jeremy, o.s. of late Henry Garnet, vicar of
Much Middlefold, Salop; author. Publications: "The
Outsider", "The Manoeuvres of Arthur". Hobbies:
Cricket, football, swimming, golf. Clubs: Arts.'

But if you search among the Us for Ukridge,
Stanley Featherstonehaugh, details of whose

tempestuous career would make really interesting reading, you find no mention of him. It seems unfair, though I imagine Ukridge bears it with fortitude. That much-enduring man has had a lifetime's training in bearing things with fortitude.

He seemed in his customary jovial spirits now, as he dashed into the room, clinging on to the pince-nez which even ginger-beer wire rarely kept stable for two minutes together.

'My dear old man,' he shouted, springing at me and seizing my hand in a grip like the bite of a horse. 'How *are* you, old buck? This is good. By Jove, this is fine, what?'

He dashed to the door and looked out.

'Come on, Millie! Pick up the waukeesis. Here's old Garnet, looking just the same as ever. Devilish handsome fellow! You'll be glad you came when you see him. Beats the zoo hollow!'

There appeared round the corner of Ukridge a young woman. She paused in the doorway and smiled pleasantly.

'Garny, old horse,' said Ukridge with some pride, 'this is *her!* The pride of the home. Companion of joys and sorrows and all the rest of it. In fact,' in a burst of confidence, 'my wife.'

I bowed awkwardly. The idea of Ukridge married was something too overpowering to be readily assimilated.

'Buck up, old horse,' said Ukridge, encouragingly. He had a painful habit of addressing all and sundry by that title. In his schoolmaster days—at one period of his vivid career he and I had been colleagues on the staff of a private school—he had made use of it while interviewing the parents of new pupils, and the latter had gone away, as a rule, with a feeling that his must be either the easy manner of Genius or due to alcohol, and hoping for the best. He also used it with perfect strangers in the streets, and on one occasion had been heard to address a bishop by that title, rendering that dignitary, as Mr Baboo Jaberjee would put it, sotto voce with gratification. 'Surprised to find me married, what? Garny, old boy'—sinking his voice to a whisper almost inaudible on the other side of the street—'take my tip. Go and jump off the dock yourself. You'll feel another man. Give up this bachelor business. It's a mug's game. I look on you bachelors as excrescences on the social system. I regard you, old man, purely and simply as a wart. Go and get married, laddie, go and get married. By gad, I've forgotten to pay the cabby. Lend me a couple of bob, Garny old chap.'

He was out of the door and on his way downstairs before the echoes of his last remark had ceased to shake the window. I was left to entertain Mrs Ukridge.

So far her share in the conversation had been confined to the pleasant smile which was apparently her chief form of expression. Nobody talked very much when Ukridge was present. She sat on the edge of the armchair, looking very small and quiet. I was conscious of feeling a benevolent pity for her. If I had been a girl, I would have preferred to marry a volcano. A little of Ukridge, as his former headmaster had once said in a moody, reflective voice, went a very long way.

'You and Stanley have known each other a long time, haven't you?' said the object of my commiseration, breaking the silence.

'Yes. Oh yes. Several years. We were masters at the same school.'

Mrs Ukridge leaned forward with round, shining eyes.

'Really? Oh, how nice!' she said ecstatically.

Not yet, to judge from her expression and the tone of her voice, had she found any disadvantages attached to the arduous position of being Mrs Stanley Ukridge.

'He's a wonderfully versatile man,' I said.

'I believe he could do anything.'

'He'd have a jolly good try!'

'Have you ever kept fowls?' asked Mr Ukridge, with apparent irrelevance.

I had not. She looked disappointed.

'I was hoping you might have had some experience. Stanley, of course, can turn his hand to anything; but I think experience is rather a good thing, don't you?'

'Yes. But . . .'

'I have bought a shilling book called *Fowls and All about Them*, and this week's copy of *C.A.C.*'

'*C.A.C.?*'

'*Chiefly about Chickens*. It's a paper, you know. But it's all rather hard to understand. You see, we . . . but here is Stanley. He will explain the whole thing.'

'Well, Garny, old horse,' said Ukridge, re-entering the room after another energetic passage of the stairs. 'Years since I saw you. Still buzzing along?'

'Still, so to speak, buzzing,' I assented.

'I was reading your last book the other day.'

'Yes?' I said, gratified. 'How did you like it?'

'Well, as a matter of fact, laddie, I didn't get beyond the third page, because the scurvy knave at the bookstall said he wasn't running a free library, and in one way and another there was a certain amount of unpleasantness. Still, it seemed bright and interesting up to page three. But let's settle down and talk business. I've got a scheme for you, Garny old man. Yessir, the idea of a thousand years. Now listen to me for a moment. Let me get a word in edgeways.'

He sat down on the table, and dragged up a chair as a leg rest. Then he took off his pince-nez, wiped them, readjusted the ginger-beer wire behind his ears, and, having hit a brown patch on the knee of his grey flannel trousers several times, in the apparent hope of removing it, resumed:

'About fowls.'

The subject was beginning to interest me. It showed a curious tendency to creep into the conversation of the Ukridge family.

'I want you to give me your undivided attention for a moment. I was saying to my wife, as we came here, "Garnet's the man! Clever devil, Garnet. Full of ideas." Didn't I, Millie?'

27

'Yes, dear.'

'Laddie,' said Ukridge impressively, 'we are going to keep fowls.'

He shifted himself farther on to the table and upset the ink pot.

'Never mind,' he said, 'it'll soak in. It's good for the texture. Or am I thinking of tobacco ash on the carpet? Well, never mind. Listen to me! When I said that we were going to keep fowls, I didn't mean in a small, piffling sort of way—two cocks and a couple of hens and a golf ball for a nest egg. We are going to do it on a large scale. We are going to run a chicken farm!'

'A chicken farm,' echoed Mrs Ukridge with an affectionate and admiring glance at her husband.

'Ah,' I said, feeling my responsibilities as chorus. 'A chicken farm.'

'I've thought it all over, laddie, and it's as clear as mud. No expenses, large profits, quick returns. Chickens, eggs, and the money streaming in faster than you can bank it. Winter and summer underclothing, my bonny boy, lined with crackling Bradbury's. It's the idea of a lifetime. Now listen to me for a moment. You get your hen—'

'One hen?'

'Call it one for the sake of argument. It makes my calculations clearer. Very well, then. Harriet the hen—you get her. Do you follow me so far?'

'Yes. You get a hen.'

'I told you Garnet was a dashed bright fellow,' said Ukridge approvingly to his attentive wife. 'Notice the way he keeps right after one's ideas? Like a bloodhound. Well, where was I?'

'You'd just got a hen.'

'Exactly. The hen. Priscilla the pullet. Well, it lays an egg every day of the week. You sell the eggs, six for half a crown. Keep of hen costs nothing. Profit—at least a couple of bob on every dozen eggs. What do you think of that?'

'I think I'd like to overhaul the figures in case of error.'

'Error!' shouted Ukridge, pounding the table till

it groaned. 'Error? Not a bit of it. Can't you follow a simple calculation like that? Oh, I forgot to say that you get—and here is the nub of the thing—you get your first hen on tick. Anybody will be glad to let you have a hen on tick. Well, then, you let this hen—this first, original hen, this on-tick hen—you let it set and hatch chickens. Now follow me closely. Suppose you have a dozen hens. Very well, then. When each of the dozen has a dozen chickens, you send the old hens back to the chappies you borrowed them from, with thanks for kind loan; and there you are, starting business with a hundred and forty-four free chickens to your name. And after a bit, when the chickens grow up and begin to lay, all you have to do is to sit back in your chair and endorse the big cheques. Isn't that so, Millie?'

'Yes, dear.'

'We've fixed it all up. Do you know Combe Regis, in Dorsetshire? On the borders of Devon. Bathing. Sea air. Splendid scenery. Just the place for a chicken farm. A friend of Millie's—girl she knew at school—has lent us a topping old house, with large grounds. All we've got to do is to get in the fowls. I've ordered the first lot. We shall find them waiting for us when we arrive.'

'Well,' I said, 'I'm sure I wish you luck. Mind you let me know how you get on.'

'Let you know!' roared Ukridge. 'Why, my dear old horse, you're coming with us.'

'Am I?' I said blankly.

'Certainly you are. We shall take no refusal. Will we, Millie?'

'No, dear.'

'Of course not. No refusal of any sort. Pack up tonight and meet us at Waterloo tomorrow.'

'It's awfully good of you . . .'

'Not a bit of it—not a bit of it. This is pure business. I was saying to Millie as we came along that you were the very man for us. A man with your flow of ideas will be invaluable on a chicken farm. Absolutely invaluable. You see,' proceeded Ukridge, 'I'm one of those practical fellows. The hard-headed type. I go straight ahead, following my nose. What you want in a business of this sort is a touch of the dreamer to help out the practical mind. We look to you for suggestions, laddie. Flashes of inspiration and all that sort of thing. Of course, you take your share of the profits. That's understood. Yes, yes, I must insist. Strict business between friends. Now, taking it that, at a conservative estimate, the net profits for the first fiscal year amount to—five thousand . . . No, better be on the safe side—say, four thousand five hundred pounds . . . But we'll arrange all that end of it when we get down there. Millie will look after that. She's the secretary of the concern. She's been writing letters to people asking for hens. So you see it's a thoroughly organized business. How many hen-letters did you write last week, old girl?'

'Ten, dear.'

Ukridge turned triumphantly to me.

'You hear? Ten. Ten letters asking for hens. That's the way to succeed. Push and enterprise.'

'Six of them haven't answered, Stanley, dear, and the rest refused.'

'Immaterial,' said Ukridge with a grand gesture. 'That doesn't matter. The point is that the letters were written. It shows we are solid and practical. Well now, can you get your things ready by tomorrow, Garny old horse?'

Strange how one reaches an epoch-making moment in one's life without recognizing it. If I had refused that invitation, I would not have— at any rate, I would have missed a remarkable experience. It is not given to everyone to see Stanley Featherstonehaugh Ukridge manage a chicken farm.

'I was thinking of going somewhere where I could get some golf,' I said undecidedly.

'Combe Regis is just the place for you, then. Perfect hotbed of golf. Full of the finest players. Can't throw a brick without hitting an amateur champion. Grand links at the top of the hill not half a mile from the farm. Bring your clubs. You'll be able to play in the afternoons. Get through serious work by lunchtime.'

'You know,' I said, 'I am absolutely inexperienced as regards fowls. I just know enough to help myself to bread sauce when I see one, but no more.'

'Excellent! You're just the man. You will bring to the work a mind unclouded by theories. You will act solely by the light of your intelligence. And you've got lots of that. That novel of yours showed the most extraordinary intelligence—at least as far as that blighter at the bookstall would let me read. I wouldn't have a professional chicken farmer about the place if he paid to come. If he applied to me, I should simply send him away. Natural intelligence is what we want. Then we can rely on you?'

'Very well,' I said slowly. 'It's very kind of you to ask me.'

'Business, laddie, pure business. Very well, then. We shall catch the eleven-twenty at Waterloo. Don't miss it. Look out for me on the platform. If I see you first, I'll shout.'

2

Holiday Reading: Classics and Comics

After I lost my father I continued my schooling in Simla, at Bishop Cotton's, but for my winter holidays I would come to my mother's and stepfather's home in Dehradun.

'Home' was never in the same place. Problems with the rent and unrelenting landlords were constantly plaguing them, and every time I came down from the hills I would find them in a different house—one of those being a rather dilapidated old bungalow on the Eastern Canal Road.

Here, I was given a room of my own, a rather gloomy room with a roof that leaked badly; but at least it was my own room, and most of the time I was left to my own devices, my mother and stepfather having given up trying to turn me into a great shikari.

That year I had come down from school with two or three books given to me as prizes—for literature or history, if I remember rightly. One was *The Complete Works of William Shakespeare*, and I decided that—having little else to do—I would read right through the plays, every one of them, as well as the poems and sonnets. This task I accomplished within a month. I can't say I enjoyed the exercise, the Elizabethan vocabulary and style being something of a deterrent, but two or three of the plays did take my fancy—*The Tempest*, *A Midsummer Night's Dream* and *King Henry V*. I had just seen Laurence Olivier's film *Henry V*, and this helped the written word come alive for me. Shakespeare needs to be performed— and performed well—to be appreciated. I even ploughed through the long narrative poem, 'The Rape of Lucrece', but it failed to excite me; I suspect that it was written by someone else.

One stormy night, with thunder and lightning at play, and the roof leaking in several places, I found it difficult to sleep. Mugs, pots and pans had been placed around the room to receive the dripping rainwater. Fortunately, we did not have power cuts in those times, so I was able to keep the light on.

The book that came to hand was Emily Brontë's *Wuthering Heights*, the perfect choice for a night of gusty winds and driving rain. And the story and the writing held me so compellingly that I stayed up to about three or four in the morning in order to finish the book. The intensity of the writing, the passion and conflict inherent in the story and its characters, captured the imagination of its thirteen-year-old reader as no other book (barring *David Copperfield*) had done till then.

Last month, some sixty-five years after first reading *Wuthering Heights*, I turned to it again, to see if it still gave out the same passion and power. And once again, I was up all night, unable to stop reading until the very end. There are not many books that can stand up to a second reading after a gap of many years. Some of Conrad's stories have stood up to this test. *Typhoon* and *Heart of Darkness* still hold me in their thrall. Favourite passages from Dickens can be enjoyed again and again. So can humorous classics such as *The Diary of a Nobody* or *Three Men in a Boat (To Say Nothing of the Dog)* or Mark Twain's *Life on the Mississippi*. Or Kipling at his best, or a great biography such as Boswell's *The Life of Samuel Johnson*.

But to return to that leaky little room on Dehra's Eastern Canal Road.

We had a radio set, and sometimes I would listen to the BBC's General Overseas Service, to comedy programmes such as Tommy Handley's *ITMA* (*It's That Man Again*). In an interview Tommy Handley had said that *The Diary of a Nobody* was his favourite book. So I went in search of it. I couldn't find it in Dehra's two small bookshops. But two years later I located it in a Simla bookshop, in an Everyman edition, and spent all my pocket money in obtaining it. Nor was I disappointed. Whenever I read it, it has me in stitches. However, the humour is very English and not everyone finds it funny. Some years ago I lent my copy to a Polish musician, who couldn't see the humour in it. We were Poles apart, you might say.

There was a bookshop in town, long gone. The Ideal Book Depot, run by a portly gentleman who sat in a dark corner at the rear of the shop. He hated getting out of his chair. If you wanted to buy a book or magazine, you had to take it off the shelf and carry it over to him along with your money. And you had to present him with the correct amount, because he disliked having to count and hand over the change; any sort of physical effort was disagreeable. He reminded me of that fine character actor Sydney Greenstreet, a very large person who looked upon the world with some distaste in the sort of villainous roles he was given in *Casablanca* and *The Maltese Falcon*.

I could seldom afford a book, but I had enough pocket money for magazines and comics. The *Strand Magazine* was still being published and sometimes carried stories by H.E. Bates and A.E. Coppard, two very fine short-story writers. H.E. Bates's long short story, 'Alexander', about a boy's discovery of the countryside, was to make a great impression on me.

Here I would buy the *Picturegoer*, a British film magazine which kept me up to date on the latest productions, some of which made it to Dehra's two English cinema halls, the Odeon and the Orient. These were well patronized up to 1947, as Dehra had a sizeable Anglo-Indian population. Most of them left after Independence. The Orient cinema, now almost a hundred years old, is still showing pictures, sometimes soft porn emanating from clandestine studios in the south. Gone are the innocent days of Madhubala, Kishore Kumar, and Abbott and Costello.

My love of the cinema was cut short by the nine

months of boarding school that found me in Simla every year, for a stretch of eight years. True, we were allowed into town and could go to the pictures during our midterm breaks, and the school had a 16 mm projector, on which selected films were shown to us once a month. But the sound system was poor, and you couldn't make out what the actors were saying to each other, unless you were good at lip-reading.

For light entertainment, comics took the place of films. No television, no Internet in those days! But for those who did not care for books (the vast majority), there were comic-book heroes in abundance—Captain Marvel, Superman, Wonder Woman, Green Lantern, Batman and many others—all-American superheroes who had invaded India in comic-book form. Personally, I preferred the English comics, which were funny— *The Dandy, Beano, Film Fun* and *Champion* (which carried stories)—but I went along with the craze for superheroes.

43

As small boys in the prep school, some of us identified ourselves with favourite superheroes. I took on the mantle of Bulletman, whose special gift was that he could fly faster than a bullet. I was no speedster (coming an easy-going last in the marathon), but in free fights I used my head to good advantage, butting my opponent in the stomach when all else failed. So from bullet-head I became Bulletman, the hero of many a free-for-all in some corner of the school playground.

In truth, I was closer in spirit to Billy Bunter, the Fat Owl of the Remove, whose exploits (in search of food) appeared in a paper called the *Magnet*; but the *Magnet* (along with other story comics like the *Wizard* and *The Hotspur*) closed down about that time, and we were left with the superheroes.

Superman and company still rule the skies, but what happened to Bulletman? I don't see him around any more. The Phantom has survived— even Popeye, in spite of his bad spelling. But poor old Bulletman appears to have bitten the dust.

Out of prep school and into senior school, I finally left comics behind and graduated to the world of literature.

H.E. Bates

Like my other heroes (Dickens, Jerome K. Jerome, Richard Jefferies), H.E. Bates came from a working-class background, and his formal education ended when he left school. But already (since the age of fourteen) he had begun to write the short stories that were to make him famous.

He completed his first novel, *The Two Sisters*, while he was working in a warehouse on a wage of £1 a week. His publisher's letter of acceptance addressed him as 'Dear Miss Bates'—they couldn't believe that a work of such sensitivity could possibly be that of a man.

Bates found his true fulfilment as a writer with the coming of World War II. He was the first writer ever to be commissioned in the Armed

Forces, in his case the RAF, solely in order to produce short stories, and he eventually became a squadron leader. The products of these war years were bestsellers, *Fair Stood the Wind for France* (1944), as well as the very moving Flying Officer X stories which set out, with exquisite pictorial simplicity, what it was actually like to be a bomber or fighter pilot.

Later in the war, Bates visited Burma, Japan and India, experiences which resulted in the novels *The Purple Plain* (1947), *The Jacaranda Tree* (1949) and *The Scarlet Sword* (1950). They turned him into an international figure.

But it was Bates's short stories, not his novels, that influenced me as I was growing up and trying out my own wings as a story writer. The bucolic humour of his *My Uncle Silas* stories, his lyrical tales of the English countryside, stories about Alexander or the boy in 'Great Uncle Crow', or passionate love stories such as *The Triple Echo* . . . Over six hundred short stories flowed from his pen, and they can be found in collections such as *The Watercress Girl and Other Stories, Sugar for the Horse* and *The Wild Cherry Tree*. Bates's inheritance from Chekhov and the great Russian writers of the nineteenth century is clearly apparent in his novellas and short stories.

David Garnett, in a famous review, compared a typical H.E. Bates story to a Renoir painting: 'His sensitivity to beauty and to character is astonishing; it is, I think, greater than the sensibility of any other living English writer; and because of it, his work always reminds me of the painting of Renoir. His best stories have the extreme delicacy and tenderness of Renoir's paint, and do not impress by their strength so much as by their fragility.'

Other writers who had something in common with Bates, and whom I greatly admired, were Walter de la Mare, with his empathy for nature, and Rumer Godden, with her tender portrayals of India in *The River* (filmed in 1951 by Jean Renoir, son of the artist Claude Renoir), *Black Narcissus* and *Kingfishers Catch Fire*.

From *The Best of H.E. Bates*

(1944, 1980)

Great Uncle Crow

Once in the summertime, when the water lilies were in bloom and the wheat was new in ear, his grandfather took him on a long walk up the river, to see his Uncle Crow. He had heard so much of Uncle Crow, so much that was wonderful and to be marvelled at, and for such a long time, that he knew him to be, even before that, the most remarkable fisherman in the world.

'Masterpiece of a man, your Uncle Crow,' his grandfather said. 'He could git a clothes line any day and tie a brick on it and a mossel of cake and go out and catch a pike as long as your arm.'

When he asked what kind of cake his grandfather seemed irritated and said it was just like a boy to ask questions of that sort.

'Any kind o' cake,' he said. 'Plum cake. Does it matter? Caraway cake. Christmas cake if you like. Anything. I shouldn't wonder if he could catch a pretty fair pike with a cold baked tater.'

'Only a pike?'

'Times,' his grandfather said, 'I've seen him sittin' on the bank on a sweltering hot day like a furnace, when nobody was gittin' a bite not even off a bloodsucker. And there your Uncle Crow'd be a-pullin' 'em out by the dozen, like a man shellin' harvest beans.'

'And how does he come to be my Uncle Crow,' he said, 'if my mother hasn't got a brother? Nor my father.'

'Well,' his grandfather said, 'he's really your mother's own cousin, if everybody had their rights. But all on us call him Uncle Crow.'

'And where does he live?'

'You'll see,' his grandfather said. 'All by himself. In a little titty bit of a house, by the river.'

The little bit of a house, when he first saw it, surprised him very much. It was not at all unlike a black tarred boat that had either slipped down a slope and stuck there on its way to launching or one that had been washed up and left there in a flood. The roof of brown tiles had a warp in it and the sides were mostly built, he thought, of tarred beer-barrels.

The two windows with their tiny panes were about as large as chessboards and Uncle Crow had nailed underneath each of them a sill of sheet tin that was still a brilliant blue, each with the words 'Backache Pills' in white lettering on it, upside down.

On all sides of the house grew tall feathered reeds. They enveloped it like gigantic whispering corn. Some distance beyond the great reeds the river went past in a broad slow arc, on magnificent, kingly currents, full of long white islands of water lilies, as big as china breakfast cups, shining and yellow hearted in the sun.

He thought, on the whole, that that place, the river with the water lilies, the little titty bit of a house, and the great forest of reeds talking between soft brown beards, was the nicest place he had ever seen.

'Anybody about?' his grandfather called. 'Crow!—anybody at home?'

The door of the house was partly open, but at first there was no answer. His grandfather pushed open the door still farther with his foot. The reeds whispered down by the river and were answered, in the house, by a sound like the creak of bed springs.

'Who is't?'

'It's me, Crow,' his grandfather called. 'Lukey. Brought the boy over to have a look at you.'

A big, gangling, red-faced man with rusty hair came to the door. His trousers were black and very tight. His eyes were a smeary vivid blue, the same colour as the stripes of his shirt, and his trousers were kept up by a leather belt with brass escutcheons on it, like those on horses' harness.

'Thought very like you'd be out a-pikin',' his grandfather said.

'Too hot. How's Lukey boy? Ain't seed y' lately, Lukey boy.'

His lips were thick and very pink and wet, like cow's lips. He made a wonderful, erupting, jolly sound somewhat between a belch and a laugh.

'Comin' in a minute?'

In the one room of the house was an iron bed with an old red check horse-rug spread over it and a stone copper in one corner and a bare wooden table with dirty plates and cups and a tin kettle on it. Two osier baskets and a scythe stood in another corner.

Uncle Crow stretched himself full length on the bed as if he was very tired. He put his knees in the air. His belly was tight as a bladder of lard in his black trousers, which were mossy green on the knees and seat.

'How's the fishin'?' his grandfather said. 'I bin tellin' the boy—'

Uncle Crow belched deeply. From where the sun struck full on the tarred wall of the house there was a hot whiff of baking tar. But when Uncle Crow belched there was a smell like the smell of yeast in the air.

'It ain't bin all that much of a summer yit,' Uncle Crow said. 'Ain't had the rain.'

'Not like that summer you catched the big 'un down at Archer's Mill. I recollect you a-tellin' on me—'

'Too hot and dry by half,' Uncle Crow said. 'Gits in your gullet like chaff.'

'You recollect that summer?' his grandfather said. 'Nobody else a-fetching on 'em out only you—'

'Have a drop o' neck-oil,' Uncle Crow said.

The boy wondered what neck-oil was and presently, to his surprise, Uncle Crow and his grandfather were drinking it. It came out of a dark-green bottle and it was a clear, bright amber, like cold tea, in the two glasses.

'The medder were yeller with 'em,' Uncle Crow said. 'Yeller as a guinea.'

He smacked his lips with a marvellously juicy, fruity sound. The boy's grandfather gazed at the neck-oil and said he thought it would be a corker if it was kept a year or two, but Uncle Crow said, 'Trouble is, Lukey boy, it's a terrible job to keep it. You start tastin' on it to see if it'll keep and then you taste on it again and you go on tastin' on it until they ain't a drop left as 'll keep.'

Uncle Crow laughed so much that the bed springs cackled underneath his bouncing trousers.

'Why is it called neck-oil?' the boy said.

'Boy,' Uncle Crow said, 'when you git older, when you git growed up, you know what'll happen to your gullet?'

'No.'

'It'll git sort o' rusted up inside. Like a old gutter pipe. So's you can't swaller very easy. Rusty as old Harry it'll git. You know that, boy?'

'No.'

'Well, it will. I'm tellin', on y'. And you know what y' got to do then?'

'No.'

'Every now and then you gotta git a drop o' neck-oil down it. So's to ease it. A drop o' neck-oil every once in a while—that's what you gotta do to keep the rust out.'

The boy was still contemplating the curious prospect of his neck rusting up inside in later years when Uncle Crow said, 'Boy, you go outside and jis' round the corner you'll see a bucket. You bring handful o' cresses out on it. I'll bet you're hungry, ain't you?'

'A little bit.'

He found the watercress in the bucket, cool in the shadow of the little house, and when he got back inside with them Uncle Crow said:

'Now you put the cresses on that there plate there and then put your nose inside that there basin and see what's inside. What is't, eh?'

'Eggs.'

'Ought to be fourteen on 'em. Four apiece and two over. What sort are they, boy?'

'Moorhens'.'

'You got a knowin' boy here, Lukey,' Uncle Crow said. He dropped his scaly red lid of one eye like an old cockerel going to sleep. He took another drop of neck-oil and gave another fruity, juicy laugh as he heaved his body from the bed. 'A very knowin' boy.'

Presently he was carving slices of thick brown bread with a great horn-handled shut-knife and pasting each slice with summery golden butter. Now and then he took another drink of neck-oil and once he said:

'You get the salt pot, boy, and empty a bit out on that there saucer, so's we can all dip in.'

Uncle Crow slapped the last slice of bread on to the buttered pile and then said:

'Boy, you take that there jug there and go a step or two up the path and dip yourself a drop o' spring

63

water. You'll see it. It comes out of a little bit of a wall, jist by a doddle-willer.'

When the boy got back with the jug of spring water Uncle Crow was opening another bottle of neck-oil and his grandfather was saying, 'God a-mussy man, goo steady. You'll have me agooin' one way and another—'

'Man alive,' Uncle Crow said, 'and what's wrong with that?'

Then the watercress, the salt, the moorhens' eggs, the spring water, and the neck-oil were all ready. The moorhens' eggs were hard-boiled. Uncle Crow lay on the bed and cracked them with his teeth, just like big brown nuts, and said he thought the watercress was just about as nice and tender as a young lady.

'I'm sorry we ain't got the gold plate out though. I had it out a-Sunday.' He closed his old cockerel-lidded eye again and licked his tongue backwards and forwards across his lips and dipped another peeled egg in salt. 'You know what I had for my dinner a-Sunday, boy?'

'No.'

'A pussycat on a gold plate. Roasted with broad beans and new taters. Did you ever heerd talk of anybody eatin' a roasted pussycat, boy?'

'Yes.'

'You did?'

'Yes,' he said, 'that's a hare.'

'You got a very knowin' boy here, Lukey,' Uncle Crow said. 'A very knowin' boy.'

Then he screwed up a big dark-green bouquet of watercress and dipped it in salt until it was entirely frosted and then crammed it in one neat wholesale bite into his soft pink mouth.

'But not on a gold plate?' he said.

He had to admit that.

'No, not on a gold plate,' he said.

All that time he thought the fresh watercress, the moorhens' eggs, the brown bread and butter and the spring water were the most delicious, wonderful things he had ever eaten in the world. He felt that

65

only one thing was missing. It was that whenever his grandfather spoke of fishing Uncle Crow simply took another draught of neck-oil.

'When are you goin' to take us fishing?' he said.

'You 'et up that there egg,' Uncle Crow said. 'That's the last one. You 'et that there egg up and I'll tell you what.'

'What about gooin' as far as that big deep hole where the chub lay?' grandfather said. 'Up by the back brook—'

'I'll tell you what, boy,' Uncle Crow said, 'you git your grandfather to bring you over September time, of a morning, afore the steam's off the winders. Mushroomin' time. You come over and we'll have a bit o' bacon and mushroom for breakfast and then set into the pike. You see, boy, it ain't the pikin' season now. It's too hot. Too bright. It's too bright of afternoon, and they ain't a-bitin'.'

He took a long, rich swig of neck-oil.

'Ain't that it, Lukey? That's the time, ain't it, mushroom time?'

'Thass it,' his grandfather said.

'Tot out,' Uncle Crow said. 'Drink up. My throat's jist easin' orf a bit.'

He gave another wonderful belching laugh and told the boy to be sure to finish up the last of the watercress and the bread and butter. The little room was rich with the smell of neck-oil, and the tarry sun-baked odour of the beer-barrels that formed its walls. And through the door came, always, the sound of reeds talking in their beards, and the scent of summer meadows drifting in from beyond the great curl of the river with its kingly currents and its islands of full-blown lilies, white and yellow in the sun.

'I see the wheat's in ear,' his grandfather said. 'Ain't that the time for tench, when the wheat's in ear?'

'Mushroom time,' Uncle Crow said. 'That's the time. You git mushroom time here, and I'll fetch you a tench out as big as a cricket bat.'

He fixed the boy with an eye of wonderful watery, glassy blue and licked his lips with a lazy tongue, and said:

'You know what colour a tench is, boy?'

'Yes,' he said.

'What colour?'

'The colour of the neck-oil.'

'Lukey,' Uncle Crow said, 'you got a very knowin' boy here. A very knowin' boy.'

After that, when there were no more cresses or moorhens' eggs, or bread and butter to eat, and his grandfather said he'd get hung if he touched another drop of neck-oil, he and his grandfather walked home across the meadows.

'What work does Uncle Crow do?' he said.

'Uncle Crow? Work? — well, he ain't — Uncle Crow? Well, he works, but he ain't what you'd call a reg'lar worker—'

All the way home he could hear the reeds talking in their beards. He could see the water lilies that reminded him so much of the gold and white inside the moorhens' eggs. He could hear the happy sound of Uncle Crow laughing and sucking at the neck-oil, and crunching the fresh salty cresses into his mouth in the tarry little room.

He felt happy, too, and the sun was a gold plate in the sky.

3

Schooldays, Rule Days

Although I was a good football goalkeeper (not too much running around), I found most games rather boring. Cricket was one of them. Especially, when one had to turn up at the 'nets' in order to bowl endless overs at an important player who was there simply to practise his shots. And then to sit around for the better part of the day, waiting for a chance to bat, and then to be given out LBW (Leg before Wicket) by an umpire (i.e., teacher) who hated you anyway and was just waiting for a chance to get even . . . and so, before we went out to field, or in the process of running after a ball that refused to slow down, I would get a cramp in one of my legs (sometimes genuine) and leave the field, retiring to the dormitory where I would enjoy an hour or two of refreshing sleep while the rest of the team slipped and stumbled about on the stony outfield.

No grass in our school 'flats' or playing fields. As a goalkeeper, I lost a considerable amount of skin from my knees and elbows; even so, it was better than chasing cricket balls.

Elsewhere, I think I have mentioned my antipathy to running races. Why bother to come first when, with less effort, you can come in last and be none the worse for it? There is no law against coming in last. Those marathon runs took us through the town's outskirts, and along the way were numerous vendors selling roasted corn, or peanuts, or hot pakoras. Those of us who were not desirous of winning medals (they were made of tin, anyway) would stop for refreshment (making sure the teacher on duty was out of sight) and bring up the rear of the race while the poor winner, looking famished and quite exhausted, would have to wait patiently for the school dinner—usually rubbery chapattis and a curry made of undercooked potatoes and stringy 'French' beans: more string than beans.

Running wasn't my forte, but I wasn't too bad at the shot-put, and could throw that iron ball a considerable distance. The teacher who had been our cricket coach and umpire made the mistake of standing too close to me, and I dropped the shot (quite accidentally) on his toes, rendering him unfit for duty for a few days.

'Sorry, sir!' I said. 'It slipped.'

But he wasn't the forgiving type; when the boxing tournaments came around, he put me in the ring with the school's 'most scientific' boxer. Not being of a scientific bent, I threw science to the winds and used my famous headbutt to good effect. Why box for three rounds when everything can be settled in one?

Games were, of course, compulsory in most boarding schools. They were supposed to turn you into real men, even if your IQ remained at zero.

This commitment to the values of the playing fields of Eton and Rugby meant that literature came very low on that list of the school's priorities. We had a decent enough library, consisting mainly of books that had been gifted to the school; but as reading them wasn't compulsory (as opposed to boxing and cricket), the library was an island seldom inhabited except by one shipwrecked and literary young man—yours truly.

My housemaster, Mr Brown, realizing that I was a bookish boy, had the wisdom to put me in charge of the library. This meant that I had access to the keys, and that I could visit that storeroom of books whenever I liked.

The great escape!

And so, whenever I could dodge cricket nets or PT (physical training), or swimming lessons, or extra classes of any kind, I would ship away to my desert island and there, surrounded by books in lieu of coconut palms, read or write or dawdle or dream, secure in the knowledge that no one was going to disturb me, since no one else was interested in reading books.

Today, teachers and parents and the world at large complain that the reading habit is dying out, that youngsters don't read, that no one wants books. Well, all I can say is that they never did! If reading is a minority pastime today it was even more so sixty years ago. And there was no television then, no Internet, no Facebook, no tweeting and twittering, no video games, no DVD players, none of the distractions that we blame today for the decline in the reading habit.

In truth, it hasn't declined. I keep meeting young people who read, and many who want to write. This was not the case when I was a boy. If I was asked what I wanted to do after school, and I said, 'I'm going to be a writer,' everyone would laugh. Writers were eccentric creatures who lived on the moon or in some never-never land; they weren't real. So I stopped saying I was going to be a writer and instead said I was going to be a detective. Somehow, that made better sense. After all, Dick Tracy was a comic-book hero. And there was a radio series featuring Bulldog Drummond, a precursor to James Bond.

In the library, I soon had many good friends—Dickens and Chekhov and Maupassant and Barrie and Somerset Maugham and Hugh Walpole and P.G. Wodehouse and many others—yes, and even Bulldog Drummond, whose adventures were set forth by 'Sapper', whose real name was H.C. McNeile.

Pseudonyms were popular once. 'Saki' was H.H. Munro. 'O. Henry' was William Porter. 'Mark Twain' was Samuel Clemens. 'Ellery Queen' was two people.

My own favourite was 'A Modern Sinbad', who wrote some wonderful sea stories—*Spin a Yarn Sailor* (1934), a battered copy still treasured by me, full of great storms and colourful ships' captains, and sailors singing shanties; but I have never been able to discover his real name, and his few books are hard to find. Perhaps one of my young computer-friendly readers can help!

Apart from Tagore, there were very few Indian authors writing in English in the 1940s. R.K. Narayan's first book was introduced to the world by Graham Greene, Mulk Raj Anand's by E.M. Forster; they were followed in the fifties by Raja Rao, Attia Hosain, Khushwant Singh, Sudhin Ghose, G.V. Desani and Kamala Markandaya.

A few years ago, while I was sitting at my desk in Ivy Cottage (where I am sitting right now), a dapper little gentleman appeared in my doorway and introduced himself. He was none other than Mulk Raj Anand, aged ninety (he lived to be ninety-nine). He spent over an hour with me, talking about books, and I told him I'd read his novel *Coolie* while I was still at school in Simla— Simla being the setting for the novel. When he left, he thrust a ten-rupee note into little Siddharth's pocket. Siddharth, my great-grandson, was then only three or four and doesn't remember the occasion; but it was a nice gesture on the part of that Grand Old Man of Letters.

But I digress. I grow old and inclined to ramble. I should take T.S. Eliot's advice and wear the bottoms of my trousers rolled (and yes, they are beginning to look a little frayed and baggy). Is this what they call 'existential writing'? Or 'stream of consciousness'?

Back to my old school library. Yes, *my* library, since no one else seemed to bother with it. And from reading, it was only a short step to writing.

A couple of spare exercise books were soon filled with my observations on school life—friends, foes, teachers, the headmaster's buxom wife, dormitory fights, the tuck shop and the mysterious disappearance of a senior prefect who was later found 'living in sin' with a fading film star (thirty years his senior) in a villa near Sanjauli. Well, that was his great escape from the tedium of boarding-school life.

It was not long before my magnum opus fell

into the hands of my class teacher who passed it on to the headmaster, who sent for me and gave me a flogging. The exercise books were shredded and thrown into his wasterpaper basket. End of my first literary venture.

But the seed had been sown, and I was not too upset. If the world outside could accommodate other writers, it could accommodate me too. My time would come.

In the meantime, there were books and authors to be discovered. A lifetime of reading lay ahead. Old books, new books, classics, thrillers, stories short and tall, travelogues, histories, biographies, comedies, comic strips, poems, memories, fantasies, fables . . . The adventure would end only when the lights went out for ever.

'Lights out!' called the master on duty, making his rounds of the dormitories.

Out went the lights.

And out came my little pocket torch, and whatever book I was immersed in, and with my head under the blanket I would read on for another twenty or thirty minutes, until sleep overcame me.

And in that sleep what dreams would come . . . dreams crowded with a wonderful cast of characters, all jumbled up, but each one distinct and alive, coming up to me and shaking me by the hand: Mr Pickwick, Sam Weller, Aunt Betsey Trotwood, Mr Dick, Tom Sawyer, Long John Silver, Lemuel Gulliver, the Mad Hatter, Alice, Mr Toad of Toad Hall, Hercule Poirot, Jeeves, Lord Emsworth, Kim, the Lama, Mowgli, Dick Turpin, William Brown, Nero Wolfe, Ariel, Ali Baba, Snow White, Cinderella, Shakuntala, John Gilpin, Sherlock Holmes, Dr Watson, Peter and Wendy, Captain Hook, Richard Hannay, Allan Quatermain, Sexton Blake, Desperate Dan, old Uncle Tom Cobley and all.

W. Somerset Maugham

'I wanted money and I wanted fame,' wrote Somerset Maugham in a preface to one of his plays, and he achieved both in the course of a long and brilliant literary career.

He was born in 1874, attended King's School, Canterbury, and the Heidelberg University, and studied medicine in London. But he gave up medicine for literature and wrote his first novel, *Liza of Lambeth* (1897), when in his early twenties.

An avowed disciple of Anton Chekhov and Maupassant, Maugham was a realistic writer with a style that was austere and unsentimental, without frills—but always compelling.

Of Human Bondage, a masterpiece of

autobiographical fiction, came out in 1915. His travels took him to China, which resulted in *The Painted Veil*; to the South Seas, which produced *The Moon and Sixpence* (based on the artist Paul Gauguin's life in Tahiti); to India, which gave him *The Razor's Edge*; to Paris, for *Christmas Holiday*; and to the Far East, which resulted in many of his greatest short stories.

But it was *Cakes and Ale* (1930), set in England, that I remember best, probably because it was my first foray into adult fiction. It was not in our school library, but it was doing the rounds amongst some of the older boys, along with Zola's *Nana* and Kathleen Winsor's *Forever Amber*. It was a thinly veiled portrait of Thomas Hardy, the grand old man of English letters; but it was the character of Rosie, his young and effervescent wife, that appealed to the adolescent reader. I read the novel again last month, and found that it had lost none of its freshness and appeal. 'Enjoy yourself while you have the chance, I say,' says

Rosie. 'We shall all be dead in a hundred years and what will anything matter then?'

Amongst Maugham's other works there are two books that are essential reading for any would-be writer. These are *The Summing Up* and *A Writer's Notebook*. They are not on my shelf simply because, whenever I manage to get copies, some aspiring young writer comes along and makes off with them!

From *Cakes and Ale* (1930)

by W. Somerset Maugham

Chapter 15

Edward Driffield worked at night, and Rosie, having nothing to do, was glad to go out with one or other of her friends. She liked luxury and Quentin Forde was well-to-do. He would fetch her in a cab and take her to dine at Kettner's or the Savoy, and she would put on her grandest clothes for him; and Harry Retford, though he never had a bob, behaved as if he had, and took her about in hansoms, too, and gave her dinner at Romano's or in one or other of the little restaurants that were becoming modish in Soho. He was an actor and a clever one, but he was difficult to suit and so was often out of work. He was about thirty, a man with a pleasantly ugly face and a clipped way of speaking that made what he said sound funny. Rosie liked his devil-may-care attitude towards life, the swagger with which he wore clothes made by the best tailor in London and unpaid for, the recklessness with which he would put a fiver he hadn't got on a horse, and the generosity with which he flung his money about when a lucky win put him in funds. He was gay, charming, vain, boastful and unscrupulous. Rosie told me that once he had pawned his watch to take her out to dinner and then borrowed a couple of pounds from the actor-manager who had given them seats for the play in order to take him out to supper with them afterwards.

But she was just as well pleased to go with Lionel Hillier to his studio and eat a chop that he and she cooked between them and spend the evening talking, and it was only very rarely that she would dine with me at all. I used to fetch her after I had had my dinner in Vincent Square and she hers with

Driffield, and we would get on a bus and go to a music hall. We went here and there, to the Pavilion or the Tivoli, sometimes to the Metropolitan if there was a particular turn we wanted to see; but our favourite was the Canterbury. It was cheap and the show was good. We ordered a couple of beers and I smoked my pipe. Rosie looked round with delight at the great dark smoky house, crowded to the ceiling with the inhabitants of south London.

'I like the Canterbury,' she said. 'It's so homey.'

I discovered that she was a great reader. She liked history, but only history of a certain kind, the lives of queens and of mistresses of royal personages; and she would tell me with a childlike wonder of the strange things she read. She had a wide acquaintance with the six consorts of King Henry VIII and there was little she did not know about Mrs Fitzherbert and Lady Hamilton. Her appetite was prodigious and she ranged from Lucrezia Borgia to the wives of Philip of Spain; then there was the long list of the royal mistresses of France. She knew them all, and all about them, from Agnes Sorel down to Madame du Barry.

'I like to read about real things,' she said. 'I don't much care for novels.'

She liked to gossip about Blackstable, and I thought it was on account of my connection with it that she liked to come out with me. She seemed to know all that was going on there.

'I go down every other week or so to see my mother,' she said. 'Just for the night, you know.'

'To Blackstable?'

I was surprised.

'No, not to Blackstable,' Rosie smiled. 'I don't know that I'd care to go there just yet. To Haversham. Mother comes over to meet me. I stay at the hotel where I used to work.'

She was never a great talker. Often when, the night being fine, we decided to walk back from the music hall at which we had been spending the evening, she never opened her mouth. But her silence was intimate and comfortable. It did not exclude you; it included you in a pervasive well-being.

I was talking about her once to Lionel Hillier and I said to him that I could not understand how she had turned from the fresh, pleasant-looking young woman I had first known at Blackstable into the lovely creature whose beauty now practically everyone acknowledged. (There were people who made reservations. 'Of course she has a very good figure,' they said, 'but it's not the sort of face I very much admire personally.' And other said: 'Oh, yes, a very pretty woman; but it's a pity she hasn't a little more distinction.')

'I can explain that to you in half a jiffy,' said Lionel Hillier. 'She was only a fresh buxom wench when you first met her. *I* made her beauty.'

I forget what my answer was, but I know it was ribald.

'All right. That just shows you don't know anything about beauty. No one ever thought very much of Rosie till I saw her like the sun shining silver. It wasn't till I painted it that anyone knew that her hair was the most lovely thing in the world.'

'Did you make her neck and her breasts and her carriage and her bones?' I asked.

'Yes, damn you, that's just what I did do.'

When Hillier talked of Rosie in front of her she listened to him with a smiling gravity. A little flush came into her pale cheeks. I think that first when he spoke to her of her beauty she believed he was just making game of her; but when she found out that he wasn't, when he painted her silvery gold, it had no particular effect on her. She was a trifle amused, pleased, of course, and a little surprised, but it did not turn her head. She thought him a little mad. I often wondered whether there was anything between them. I could not forget all I had heard of Rosie at Blackstable and what I had seen in the vicarage garden; I wondered about Quentin Forde, too, and Harry Retford. I used to watch them with her. She was not exactly familiar with them, comradely rather; she used to make her appointments with them quite openly in anybody's hearing; and when she looked at them it was with that mischievous, childlike smile which I had now discovered held such a mysterious beauty. Sometimes when we were sitting side by side in a music hall I looked at her face; I do not think I was in love with her, I merely enjoyed the sensation of sitting quietly beside her and looking at the pale gold of her hair and the pale gold of her skin. Of course Lionel Hillier was right; the strange thing was that this gold did give one a strange moonlight feeling. She had the serenity of a summer evening when the light fades slowly from the unclouded sky. There was nothing dull in her immense placidity; it was as living as the sea when under the August sun it lay calm and shining along the Kentish coast. She reminded me of a sonatina by an old Italian composer with its wistfulness in which there is yet an urbane flippancy and its light rippling gaiety in which echoes still the trembling of a sigh. Sometimes, feeling my eyes on her, she would turn round and for a moment or two look me full in the face. She did not speak. I did not know of what she was thinking.

Once, I remember, I fetched her at Limpus Road, and the maid, telling me she was not ready, asked me to wait in the parlour. She came in. She was in black velvet, with a picture hat covered with ostrich feathers (we were going to the Pavilion and she had dressed up for it), and she looked so lovely that it took my breath away. I was staggered. The clothes of that day gave a woman dignity, and there was something amazingly attractive in the way her virginal beauty (sometimes she looked like the exquisite statue of Psyche in the museum at Naples) contrasted with the stateliness of her gown. She had a trait that I think must be very rare: the skin under her eyes, faintly blue, was all dewy. Sometimes I could not persuade myself that it was natural, and once I asked her if she had rubbed Vaseline under her eyes. That was just the effect it gave. She smiled, took a handkerchief, and handed it to me.

'Rub them and see,' she said.

Then one night when we had walked home from the Canterbury, and I was leaving her at her door, when I held out my hand she laughed a little, a low chuckle it was, and leaned forward.

'You old silly,' she said.

She kissed me on the mouth. It was not a hurried peck, nor was it a kiss of passion. Her lips, those very full red lips of hers, rested on mine long enough for me to be conscious of their shape and their warmth and their softness. Then she withdrew them, but without hurry, in silence pushed open the door, skipped inside and left me. I was so startled that I had not been able to say anything. I accepted her kiss stupidly. I remained inert. I turned away and walked back to my lodgings. I seemed to hear still in my ears Rosie's laughter. It was not contemptuous or wounding, but frank and affectionate; it was as though she laughed because she was fond of me.

99

Chapter 16

I did not go out with Rosie again for more than a week. She was going down to Haversham to spend a night with her mother. I had various engagements in London. Then she asked me if I would go to the Haymarket Theatre with her. The play was a success and free seats were not to be had, so we made up our minds to go in the pit. We had a steak and a glass of beer at the Café Monico and then stood with the crowd. In those days there was no orderly queue and when the doors were opened there was a mad rush and scramble to get in. We were hot and breathless and somewhat battered when at last we pushed our way into our seats.

We walked back through St James's Park. The night was so lovely that we sat down on a bench. In the starlight Rosie's face and her fair hair glowed softly. She was suffused, as it were (I express it awkwardly, but I do not know how to describe the emotion she gave me), with a friendliness at once candid and tender. She was like a silvery flower of the night that only gave its perfume to the moonbeams. I slipped my arm round her waist and she turned her face to mine. This time it was I who kissed. She did not move; her soft red lips submitted to the pressure of mine with a calm, intensive passivity as the water of a lake accepts the light of the moon. I don't know how long we stayed there.

'I'm awfully hungry,' she said suddenly.

'So am I,' I laughed.

'Couldn't we go and have some fish and chips somewhere?'

'Rather.'

In those days I knew my way very well about Westminster, not yet a fashionable quarter for parliamentary and otherwise cultured persons, but slummy and down at heel; and after we had come out of the park, crossing Victoria Street, I led Rosie to a fried-fish shop in Horseferry Row. It was late and the only other person there was the driver of a four-wheeler waiting outside. We ordered our fish and chips and a bottle of beer. A poor woman came in and bought two penn'orth of mixed and took it away with her in a piece of paper. We ate with appetite.

Our way back to Rosie's led through Vincent Square and as we passed my house I asked her:

'Won't you come in for a minute? You've never seen my rooms.'

'What about your landlady? I don't want to get you into trouble.'

'Oh, she sleeps like a rock.'

'I'll come in for a little.'

I slipped my key into the lock and, because the

passage was dark, took Rosie's hand to lead her in. I lit the gas in my sitting room. She took off her hat and vigorously scratched her head. Then she looked for a glass, but I was very artistic and had taken down the mirror that was over the chimney piece and there was no means in the room for anyone to see what he looked like.

'Come into my bedroom,' I said. 'There's a glass there.'

I opened the door and lit the candle. Rosie followed me in and I held it up so that she should be able to see herself. I looked at her in the glass as she arranged her hair. She took two or three pins out, which she put in her mouth, and taking one of my brushes, brushed her hair up from the nape of her neck. She twisted it, patted it, and put back the pins, and as she was intent on this her eyes caught mine in the glass and she smiled at me. When she had replaced the last pin she turned and faced me; she did not say anything; she looked at me tranquilly still with that little friendly smile in

103

her blue eyes. I put down the candle. The room was very small and the dressing table was by the bed. She raised her hand and softly stroked my cheek.

I wish now that I had not started to write this book in the first-person singular. It is all very well when you can show yourself in an amiable or touching light, and nothing can be more effective than the modest heroic or pathetic humorous which in this mode is much cultivated; it is charming to write about yourself when you see on the reader's eyelash the glittering tear and on his lips the tender smile; but it is not so nice when you have to exhibit yourself as a plain damned fool.

A little while ago I read in the *Evening Standard* an article by Mr Evelyn Waugh in the course of which he remarked that to write novels in the first person was a contemptible practice. I wish he had explained why, but he merely threw out the statement with just the same take-it-or-leave-it casualness as Euclid used when he made his celebrated observation about parallel straight lines. I was much concerned, and forthwith asked Alroy Kear (who reads everything, even the books he writes prefaces for) to recommend to me some works on the art of fiction. On his advice I read the *Craft of Fiction* by Mr Percy Lubbock, from which I learned that the only way to write novels was like Henry James; after that I read *Aspects of the Novel* by Mr E.M. Forster, from which I learned that the only way to write novels was like Mr E.M. Forster; then I read *The Structure of the Novel* by Mr Edwin Muir, from which I learned nothing at all. In none of them could I discover anything to the point at issue. All the same I can find one reason why certain novelists, such as Defoe, Sterne, Thackeray, Dickens, Emily Brontë and Proust, well known in their day but now doubtless forgotten, have used the method that Mr Evelyn Waugh reprehends. As we grow older we become more conscious of the complexity, incoherence and unreasonableness of human beings; this indeed is the only excuse that offers for the middle-aged or elderly writer, whose thoughts should more properly be turned to graver matters, occupying himself with the trivial concerns of imaginary people. For if the proper study of mankind is man it is evidently more sensible to occupy yourself with the coherent, substantial and significant creatures of fiction than with the irrational and shadowy figures of real life. Sometimes the novelist feels himself like God and is prepared to tell you everything about his characters; sometimes, however, he does not; and then he tells you not everything that is to be known about them but the little he knows himself; and since as we grow older we feel ourselves less and less like God I should not be surprised to learn that with advancing years the novelist grows less and less inclined to describe more than his own experience has given him. The first-person singular is a very useful device for this limited purpose.

Rosie raised her hand and softly stroked my face. I do not know why I should have behaved as I then did; it was not at all how I had seen myself behaving on such an occasion. A sob broke from my tight throat. I do not know whether it was because I was shy and lonely (not lonely in the body, for I spent all day at the hospital with all kinds of people, but lonely in the spirit) or because my desire was so great, but I began to cry. I felt terribly ashamed of myself; I tried to control myself, I couldn't; the tears welled up in my eyes and poured down my cheeks. Rosie saw them and gave a little gasp.

'Oh, honey, what is it? What's the matter? Don't. Don't!'

She put her arms round my neck and began to cry too, and she kissed my lips and my eyes and my wet cheeks. She undid her bodice and lowered my head till it rested on her bosom. She stroked my smooth face. She rocked me back and forth as though I were a child in her arms. I kissed her breasts and I kissed the white column of her neck; and she slipped out of her bodice and out of her skirt and her petticoats and I held her for a moment by her corseted waist; then she undid it, holding her breath for an instant to enable her to do so, and stood before me in her shift. When I put my hand on her sides I could feel the ribbing of the skin from the pressure of the corsets.

'Blow out the candle,' she whispered.

It was she who awoke me when the dawn peering through the curtains revealed the shape of the bed and of the wardrobe against the darkness of the lingering night. She woke me by kissing me on the mouth and her hair falling over my face tickled me.

'I must get up,' she said. 'I don't want your landlady to see me.'

'There's plenty of time.'

Her breasts when she leaned over me were heavy on my chest. In a little while she got out of bed. I lit the candle. She turned to the glass and tied up her hair and then she looked for a moment at her naked body. Her waist was naturally small; though so well developed she was very slender; her breasts were straight and firm and they stood out from the chest as though carved in marble. It was a body made for the act of love. In the light of the candle, struggling now with the increasing day, it was all silvery gold; and the only colour was the rosy pink of the hard nipples.

We dressed in silence. She did not put on her corsets again, but rolled them up and I wrapped them in a piece of newspaper. We tiptoed along the passage and when I opened the door and we stepped out into the street the dawn ran to meet us like a cat leaping up the steps. The square was empty; already the sun was shining on the eastern windows. I felt as young as the day. We walked arm in arm till we came to the corner of Limpus Road.

'Leave me here,' said Rosie. 'One never knows.'

I kissed her and I watched her walk away. She walked rather slowly, with the firm tread of the country woman who likes to feel the good earth under her feet, and held herself erect. I could not go back to bed. I strolled on till I came to the

109

Embankment. The river had the bright hues of the early morning. A brown barge came down stream and passed under Vauxhall Bridge. In a dinghy two men were rowing close to the side. I was hungry.

4

That Year in Jersey

It's a period of my life that I haven't written about very often, not because it was unimportant or uneventful, but because no one else seemed to be interested in what I did there. And yet, looking back, I realize that it was a very formative period of my life, and that the decisions that I made there were to affect me, as a person and as a reader, in the years to come.

A year after finishing school, I had left India without too much regret, having every intention of settling in the UK and making some sort of future for myself there. I arrived in Jersey, the largest of the Channel Islands, with empty pockets and a trunk full of clothes. I was to stay with my aunt (my mother's eldest sister) who had left India just after Independence, along with her husband (a retired surgeon) and three sons, making a home in St Helier, the port and capital of the island. A number of British and Anglo-Indian exiles had settled there; the climate was tolerable, and there was no income tax.

My aunt was very keen that my mother should send her a packet of haldi, a vital ingredient in an Indian curry. Haldi and other spices were then hard to come by in post-war Britain. This was before the wave of immigration from India in the 1960s—and my aunt, who liked her curry, was desperate for a supply of haldi.

A large packet of the yellow-gold spice was placed lovingly in my clothes' trunk. But during the voyage the packet had burst open, and the haldi had scattered throughout my few clothes, staining my shirts, vests, underwear, socks and old school blazer. Haldi stains are hard, almost impossible, to eradicate. I had to borrow money from my aunt in order to buy some clothes. Worse still, most of the haldi had been lost, and we had to go weeks without a properly cooked curry.

I have always hated being dependent upon anyone for my food, lodging, clothes and books, and within a few days of my arrival I was walking the streets of St Helier, dropping in at offices and showrooms, asking for employment. This is the best way to get a job—present yourself before the boss or whoever is in charge, tell him you are prepared to do anything from making the tea to making decisions on behalf of the directors of the company—and sooner or later you will find someone who can put you to work.

During my year in Jersey, I went through four jobs, and was given the sack only once. When I grew bored with one job I simply left and found another. I did overhear my uncle talking to my aunt and saying, 'The boy has guts. He doesn't sit around waiting for something to fall into his lap.'

Well, I was seventeen and if my mentors, Charles Dickens and Jack London, could stand on their own feet while still in their teens, so could I!

The first job was with Le Riches, a large grocery store in the middle of town, where I did quite a lot of running around, carrying the day's takings from one branch to another. As this could be rather risky (the sums being quite large), they probably thought I was expendable, should someone decide to waylay me; but muggings were rare in those days, and Jersey was a very law-abiding island. Even during the German occupation (during World War II), the islanders had gone about their business (mostly fishing and growing tomatoes) without paying much heed to the occupying power. And when the war ended in Europe, the Germans simply melted away and the islanders carried on growing their tomatoes as though nothing had happened. So, don't believe everything you see in the movies.

The nice thing about running errands for Le Riches was that the last errand took me to a downmarket area called Georgetown, and there

I discovered a little cinema which specialized in showing early British comedies. And so, when I'd made my last delivery, I'd stop at the cinema and see a film before trudging through the two or three miles to my aunt's house for supper.

Here, at this little cinema hall, I made the acquaintance of many famous comedians of the 1930s and 40s—performers whom I had previously known only in the pages of *Film Fun*, a comic of my schooldays. Max Miller ('The Cheeky Chappie'), Sydney Howard, Tommy Trinder, Will Hay, George Formby (the 'Ukulele Man'), Gracie Fields ('The Lancashire Lass'), and Old Mother Riley and his partner Kitty McShane—I say *his* partner because Old Mother Riley was in fact a man, a very accomplished actor called Arthur Lucan, who dressed up as an old lady and made his name as a drag artist. These old films were indeed very funny; most of the performers had been on the music halls and knew how to get their laughs. They made life tolerable for me during that restless year when all

I wanted to do was make enough money to get back to India!

Le Riches was paying me a pittance (less than £3 a week), so when another job offer came my way, I accepted it with alacrity. The travel agents Thomas Cook & Sons had just sent a representative to Jersey, to open a small office to meet the demands of the increasing hordes of summer visitors from Britain. This representative, Mrs Manning (husband absent), needed someone to handle the telephone, make reservations and look after the office whenever she was out—which was often, as she was enjoying a love affair with a gentleman who sold second-hand fire extinguishers. I don't think she enjoyed it for long, because I heard later that he'd been arrested on a fraud or cheating charge; the fire extinguishers did not extinguish anything resembling a fire. But before that happened, we'd both been fired: I, by Mrs Manning for mixing up reservations (i.e., booking coloured people into hotels reserved for whites); and Mrs Manning by Thomas Cook for absenteeism and general mismanagement.

Unemployment has never been my problem. I was soon working for Jersey Electric, making out bills for the electricity-consuming public. It was a fairly large office, with some twenty clerks, but I was the only one who called the boss 'sir'. He called me into his inner office one day and said, 'Young man, I think you went to a public school.'

'I did, sir, but it was in India.'

'Interesting,' he said, and gave me a promotion.

But I did not stay long with Jersey Electric. A public exam was being held, with a view to selecting young clerks and others for the Jersey Civil Service, and on my uncle's prompting, I appeared for it, scoring heavily in English literature and general knowledge, and standing fourth out of a couple of hundred candidates on the island. This got me a job in the public health department. I had always professed to hate exams (having deliberately flunked a couple at school), yet here was I, being patted on the back by my uncle for a display of academic brilliance.

To the public health department I went, helping a senior clerk make up pay packets for the men working in Jersey's intricate sewer system. An inauspicious beginning for a career in the civil service. But my mind was really on other things.

I had written a novel—an immature but passionate thing, based on the journal I had kept during my last year in India—and I had stayed up many nights, using my aunt's tiny attic room to complete it. It had gone to a couple of London publishers and been rejected; but a third publisher gave me a reason for hope. This was Diana Athill, a junior partner with the firm of André Deutsch, a new publisher who was making his presence felt. In later years, Diana Athill was to become a highly successful writer and editor and something of a celebrity, but at the time she was very young (in her thirties, about fifteen years my senior) and as yet unknown. And I, of course, was completely unknown.

And in Jersey I had no friends. This wasn't Dehradun, India, where you could make friends with the boy next door, or with the boys playing cricket on a plot of wasteland, or someone in a shop or at the cinema or in a bus or railway compartment. At my place of work everyone was friendly, helpful. But when the office closed, everyone went his or her own way, and I would walk home alone, over the brow of the hill to my aunt's house.

A fifteen-minute walk. And it was a twenty-minute walk to the seafront. And about the same to the public library in the centre of the town.

Once again, books proved to be my best friends. I found most of the plays and poems of Rabindranath Tagore, an enchanting book about growing up in the Santhal Parganas, *And Gazelles Leaping* by Sudhin Ghose, and Rumer Godden's novel, *The River*, set in East Bengal (now

Bangladesh). These and other books took me back to India and gave an impetus to my own writing, so that the friends of my youth took on a new dimension in the novel I was writing.*

And then came the film adaptation of *The River*, a cinematic poem made by the great French director, Jean Renoir, son of the great painter Claude Renoir. This lyrical adaptation of Rumer Godden's novel renewed all my longings for India, and made me determined to return as soon as I could without becoming a liability for my friends and family. They would support a schoolboy but not a young man without any qualifications or prospects.

So I walked along the seafront whenever I could, watching the tide come in and the waves crashing against the sea wall, dreaming of becoming a successful writer and a master of my own fate. The sea was impersonal, majestic, accentuating

_____

*It was to be called *The Room on the Roof*.

my solitary state, but at the same time giving me a feeling of unique individuality, as I stood there alone in the darkness.

One Saturday afternoon after work I found the tide had gone out, far out, and in my bathing trunks I followed the receding waves across almost a mile of sand and rocky outcrops. I found a solitary rock, left exposed by the receding tide, and I lay down upon it in the autumn sunshine, and fell asleep. I woke to find the tide coming in again. Water was lapping around the base of the rock. It wasn't very deep, but the tide was coming in again, relentlessly, and I made for the shore with some urgency. The incoming waves aided me in my flight. I could swim a little but I did not trust the pull of the rip tide. So I blundered ashore in a bit of a panic. And when I looked back, there was no sign of my rock. It had been submerged. Perhaps I was destined to be something other than being a clerk in the public health department; or was I getting egoistic enough to think so!

London beckoned—as it had beckoned Master Copperfield, young Mr Nickleby, Dick Whittington, James Boswell, and other heroes of my bookish boyhood. Having grown up in India with the novels of Dickens, J.B. Priestley, Somerset Maugham and P.G. Wodehouse, my vision of London was very different from its post-war reality; but I was determined to give it a try.

I don't think my aunt and uncle and cousins were too sorry to see me leave. I hadn't been a nuisance or a liability—I had always handed over half my salary as my small contribution to household expenses—but nor was I an exemplary addition to their family. It was obvious to all that my heart and soul were elsewhere.

I wasn't going to lug a large tin trunk any more, with or without haldi. I bought a cheap suitcase, and stuffed it with my books, manuscripts and few clothes. The copy of *The Pickwick Papers* that I had picked up in Granny's Dehradun house went into it, along with Richard Jefferies's *The Story of My*

Heart, which I had discovered in Jersey.

I was to spend two eventful years in London before returning to India.

The cheap suitcase served me well. It is still with me today, sixty years later, a repository for old manuscripts and notebooks. Like me, it's a bit battered but still functioning.

And I still have my Pickwick and *The Story of My Heart*.

Charles Dickens

For me, Charles Dickens was, and always will be, the greatest novelist in the English language, and for one simple reason. When I was twelve, I discovered *David Copperfield*, read it right through (complete and unabridged) whenever the routine life of a boarding school permitted, and decided I was going to be a writer. And in a single-minded, determined, Dickensian sort of way, I became one. Not a major writer, but one for whom literature was religion.

Before I was fifteen I'd read *Oliver Twist*, *The Pickwick Papers*, *A Tale of Two Cities*, *Nicholas Nickleby*, *Sketches by Boz*, and the unfashionable *Barnaby Rudge*. I still dip into *The Pickwick Papers* from time to time; it's an antidote for depression and various other ailments.

I have read *Copperfield* several times, for the sheer joy of its youthful exuberance. And recently I read *Our Mutual Friend* for the first time. London's dockland came to life again for me.

I don't think Dickens ever wrote a bad novel; certainly not a dull one. He was consistently brilliant, from the time he took up his pen to create Mr Pickwick and friends to the time in his fifties when he collapsed in the middle of writing *The Mystery of Edwin Drood*. His greatest novel? The fact that no one seems to agree on it implies that they are all great in their different ways: *Bleak House* the most mature; *The Old Curiosity Shop* the most moving; *A Christmas Carol* the most exuberant; *Hard Times* the most powerful in terms of exposing social injustices; *Great Expectations* the most dramatic; *Dombey and Son* the most innovative. Every lover of Dickens will have his or her favourite. Sometimes our choice may be influenced by external factors, such as the many outstanding films that have been based upon the novels, for the characters, themes and situations lend themselves to dramatic treatment. Dickens himself was a powerful orator, whose readings made him personally popular on both sides of the Atlantic. In his wonderful voice he could, by turn, be Micawber, or Sam Weller, or Scrooge, or Marley's ghost, or Mrs Gamp. 'What a face is his to meet in a drawing room!' exclaimed the writer Leigh Hunt. 'It has the life and soul in it of fifty human beings.'

This energy, this light and motion, comes through in all his books, and especially in my own favourite. 'In *David Copperfield*,' wrote Virginia Woolf, 'characters swarm and life flows through into every creek and cranny, some common feeling—youth, gaiety, hope—envelops the tumult, brings the scattered parts together, and invests the most perfect of all the Dickens novels with an atmosphere of beauty.'

From *The Pickwick Papers* (1837)

by Charles Dickens

To ladies and gentlemen who are not in the habit of devoting themselves practically to the science of penmanship, writing a letter is no easy task; it being always considered necessary in such cases for the writer to recline his head on his left arm, so as to place his eyes as nearly as possible on a level with the paper, and, while glancing sideways at the letters he is constructing, to form with his tongue imaginary characters to correspond. These motions, although unquestionably of the greatest assistance to original composition, retard in some degree the progress of the writer; and Sam had unconsciously been a full hour and a half writing words in small text, smearing out letters with his little finger, and putting in new ones which required going over very often to render them visible through the old blots, when he was roused by the opening of the door and the entrance of his parent.

'Vell, Sammy,' said the father.

'Vell, my Prooshan Blue,' responded the son, laying down his pen. 'What's the last bulletin about mother-in-law?'

'Mrs Veller passed a very good night, but is uncommon perwerse, and unpleasant this mornin'. Signed upon oath, Tony Veller, Esquire. That's the last vun as was issued, Sammy,' replied Mr Weller, untying his shawl.

'No better yet?' inquired Sam.

'All the symptoms aggerawated,' replied Mr Weller, shaking his head. 'But wot's that, you're a-doin' of? Pursuit of knowledge under difficulties, Sammy?'

'I've done now,' said Sam, with slight embarrassment. 'I've been a-writin'.'

'So I see,' replied Mr Weller. 'Not to any young 'ooman, I hope, Sammy?'

'Why it's no use a-sayin' it ain't,' replied Sam. 'It's a walentine.'

'A what!' exclaimed Mr Weller, apparently horror-stricken by the word.

'A walentine,' replied Sam.

'Samivel, Samivel,' said Mr Weller, in reproachful accents, 'I didn't think you'd ha' done it. Arter the warnin' you've had o' your father's wicious propensities; arter all I've said to you upon this here wery subject; arter activally seein' and bein' in the company o' your own mother-in-law, vich I should ha' thought wos a moral lesson as no man could never ha' forgotten to his dyin' day! I didn't think you'd ha' done it, Sammy, I didn't think you'd ha' done it!' These reflections were too much for the good old man. He raised Sam's tumbler to his lips and drank off its contents.

5

Those Two Years in London

I was lonely in London.

Living alone in a big city, working in an office from nine to five, and coming back to a gas fire in an empty bed-sitting room, was not what I wanted out of life. I'd go out to eat in a small cafe, then return to my room, put a sheet of paper into my small portable typewriter, and type out a page or two of my novel. It was into its second draft. And there would be a third before it finally found favour with its eventual publisher.

Diana Athill, my publisher's editor, was kind and helpful. The people in the Photax office, where I worked, were kind and friendly. My landlady was kind and solicitous. Or I should say landladies, because I had at least three of them, one after another—Belsize Park, Haverstock Hill, Swiss Cottage—all Jewish landladies, widows I think, who never troubled or scolded me if I came in late or played my radio too loudly. One of them gave me breakfast with my room. Scrambled eggs and occasionally a kipper. This helped sustain me, because for lunch—at a snack bar near the office—it was almost always baked beans on toast, the cheapest item on their menu.

People were kind.

But I was lonely.

I had no companions of my own age. So I went to the pictures. And once a month to the theatre. And I dropped in at Foyles and bought old books. And I came home to my empty room and lit the gas fire and worked on my book.

After about six months on my own, I found I was losing vision in my right eye. It was as though I was looking at the world through a shifting cloud. I took vitamins—they had been 'discovered' only recently—and experimented with various eye drops, but the cloud only got darker and denser. So I went to a doctor, who said it needed further investigation and got me admitted to the Hampstead General Hospital. Here various specialists came to see me. One said I was suffering from malnutrition; true enough. Another said I had Eales Disease, a rare condition of the retina. A third felt it had something to do with a sluggish liver. (I'd suffered from jaundice in the past.) Tests showed that my intestines were full of amoebiasis, no doubt brought with me from India; and I was put on a course of emetine injections, which made me feel awful. Then my eye, or rather retina, was photographed by a high-intensity camera, and the resultant picture appeared in a medical journal (not my picture, only the eye); I had to wait a few years before my own mugshot appeared in a newspaper.

Once the amoeba had been vanquished, I (or rather my sick eye), was given cortisone injections, cortisone then being the wonder drug that was supposed to clear up all sorts of intractable conditions. This left my poor eye looking rather bloody and fierce, prompting one fellow patient to remark that I could have passed for the phantom of the opera.

Weakened by the emetine and various laxatives, I found myself too weak to get up in order to visit the loo, so I was given the privilege of having a bedpan. This occasioned some raillery from the others in the ward (it was a general ward with about twenty beds), who labelled me the BP Superman— the Bedpan Superman, after the British Petroleum Superman who was on all the hoardings.

I did improve rapidly, and was soon making the rounds of the ward, interviewing the other patients like a doctor on the rounds, quizzing them on their ailments and recommending purgatives and the Bedpan.

The book trolley did the rounds every day, and I read a book a day, discovering the stories of William Saroyan (*My Name is Aram* and *The Human Comedy*), Denton Welch (*A Voice through a Cloud*) and Josephine Tey (*The Daughter of Time*).

Saroyan had grown up in an Armenian immigrant community in California, and in his stories he captured the essence of small-town life in his part of the world. He won the Pulitzer Prize with his play *The Time of Your Life* and was very popular in the 1940s and '50s, but most of his work is now out of print.

Denton Welch was a promising young English writer who had a tragic accident while riding his bicycle on a country road. He was knocked down and run over by a lorry. For over a year he lingered between life and death, and during this period he managed to write his very moving account of his struggle to recover. He succumbed to his many injuries. I hope *A Voice through a Cloud* is reprinted some day. His earlier travel book, *Maiden Voyage,* should also be revisited.

Josephine Tey wrote several detective novels during her short life. In *The Daughter of Time,* the novel I read in my hospital bed, her detective,

Inspector Grant, finds himself in a hospital bed and passes the time by trying to reconstruct the murder of the Princes in the Tower, and with the help of his research assistant proves that it was King Henry VII and not King Richard III who was responsible for their deaths. A historical whodunnit, resolved without moving from the hospital bed. No fast-paced action, but suspenseful all the same.

How sad that such fine writers should be neglected or forgotten. Time and changing fashions take their toll on the best talents. Only a handful survive.

Sometimes short stories have a better chance of survival, because the good ones get picked up for inclusion in anthologies, and then get selected again and again. One of my earliest short stories, 'The Eyes Have It', is still turning up in anthologies and school readers, fifty years after it was first written. But once a novel goes out of print it is hard to revive it. And novels date very quickly. Sometimes too much extraneous matter goes into them, whereas the best short stories stick to the essentials.

When I wrote *The Room on the Roof* I had published only two or three short stories, so what was I, still a pimply and skinny youth, doing, trying to write a novel?

In a way it was a mistake, because in writing it I used up all the experience I had of life and was left with nothing for a second novel!

But it had to be written.

That last year in Dehra, before I left for England, was now so ingrained in me, so much a part of my emotional make-up, that it had to be expressed in the way I knew best—the written word. The journal had become a novel, and Somi, Krishan, Meena and the rest stayed alive for me on the printed page. Though it might never be published—and I couldn't be sure of this during the four years that various drafts shuttled between me and André Deutsch's editor, Diana Athill— the thing had been done, the catharsis had been completed, and I could think of other people, other loves, and try something different.

My editor, Diana Athill, was then a young woman in her thirties. Many years later she was to become quite a celebrity, the author of several successful autobiographies, frank and revealing and beautifully written. But when I knew her she hadn't done any writing (or none that I know of), although she was very busy assessing and introducing the work of many promising young writers, novelists such as Jack Kerouac, V.S. Naipaul. And although she did not (could not) teach me how to write (I stubbornly refused to temper my addiction to semicolons and certain Indianisms), she made me feel that I was part of her literary world, giving me gossip about other writers and telling me about the books they were publishing. I visited her at her flat in Regent's Park quite often, and even took her to see an Indian picture, *Aan* (the first to get a commercial release in London) but it was a terrible let-down, a very silly film, the sort of Bombay extravaganza that gave a completely misleading and over-romanticized conception of India. I felt more at ease introducing her to paan at a little Indian restaurant near Fitzroy Square, but I'm afraid she didn't care much for paan either. My efforts to make Diana an Indophile were not very successful. But she liked my book. 'I can see why you love India,' she said. 'It's so easy to make friends.'

But my first appearance in print (in London, that is) really came about as a result of my lengthy stay in the Hampstead General Hospital. A fellow patient, an English boy of about my age (perhaps a little younger), turned out to be a good reader, and when he was discharged he gave me a copy of a magazine for teenagers called the *Young Elizabethan*. A couple of months later, when I was back at my typewriter I sent them one of my short stories. It was published, and paid for. And even after I'd returned to India I continued to write for the *Elizabethan*, and several of my early stories appeared in it—'The Thief', 'The Long Day', 'The Big Race', 'The Stolen Daffodils', among others—until it finally closed down.

And while still in that hospital bed, I had written a piece called 'My Two Homes'—about an English boy growing up in an Indian home—and this became a talk that I gave on BBC Radio. The BBC's Home Service also ran a weekly short-story programme, and when I returned to India and started freelancing, many of my early stories found a home with them. 'The Night Train at Deoli', 'The Woman on Platform 8', and many others were read by Robert Rietty, a fine actor in radio plays. Back in Dehra, I would drop in on a friend who had a short-wave radio, and listen spellbound to my stories being beamed to me from distant London.

So my two-year stay in London was a good preparation for the years of struggle that lay ahead, when I returned to India. Although my job was a dull one, I did find time to write, to read, to visit the theatre, to wander about the streets of London (getting to know that city fairly well), and so banishing the loneliness that awaited me whenever I returned to my cold bed-sitting room.

And there were friends, too. Students mostly, who came in and out of my life at random.

Pravin, a Gujarati boy who was a little younger than me; he liked visiting pubs and night clubs! I had no idea what he was studying—I never saw him with a book—but he was the recipient of regular remittances from his father in Bombay.

Thanh, a Vietnamese, who cultivated me because he wanted to 'improve his English'; he dropped me when he discovered I spoke English with an Indian accent.

Vu-phuong, also Vietnamese, who used to tell me my fortune with tea leaves. When you finish drinking your tea, you let the tea leaves settle naturally, and the pattern they form gives you an indication of what to expect in the future. This was great fun, because it meant sharing innumerable cups of tea with Vu, with whom I fell in love. But when I asked her to marry me, she said it was not in the tea leaves.

Just as well, perhaps. If I'd been married in England (or Vietnam), I might never have returned to India.

And returning to India was still very much my first priority.

But first I had to save a little money, publish my novel, and try to see a little better with my right eye.

The best way to get to know a city is to walk all over the place. So I walked all over Soho and the West End; I walked from Primrose Hill down to Baker Street, looking for Sherlock Holmes, but couldn't find him; I walked all over East End, looking for places described by Dickens in *Oliver Twist* and *Our Mutual Friend*, but they looked very different from what I'd imagined; I walked around Kensington Gardens, looking for Peter Pan, but he must have been away in Neverland. So I went to Kew Gardens and felt quite at home in a big glass hothouse surrounded by tropical plants of every description. After that, whenever I felt homesick, I went down to Kew—not just in lilac time, but any time . . .

André Deutsch finally gave me a £50 advance on *The Room on the Roof.* I did not wait for it to be published, but bought a ticket to Bombay for £40; gave a week's notice to my kind employers who presented me with a travel bag; and went aboard the *S.S. Batory* at Southampton, accompanied by the said travel bag and my old suitcase bulging with books and a few clothes. It was March 1955 and I was twenty-one years old. I had left India to seek my fortune in the West; and now I was returning to the East to find, if not fortune, at least fulfilment of a sort.

Although I was over twenty, and had been earning my own living for over three years, in many ways I was still a boy, with a boy's thoughts and dreams—dreams of romance and high adventure and good companionship. And I was still a lonely boy, alone on that big ship—passengers and crew all strangers to me—sailing into an uncertain future.

I had two books with me —Thoreau's *Walden* and Richard Jefferies's *The Story of My Heart*—both reflecting my burgeoning interest in the natural world—but during the day the cabin was hot and stuffy, and the decks too crowded, so I postponed most of my reading until the journey was over. But at night, when it was cool on deck, and most of the passengers were down below, watching a film or drinking Polish vodka (the *Batory* was a Polish ship), I would sit out under the stars while the ship ploughed on through the Red Sea bringing me home to India. There was no sound but the dull thunder of the ship's screws and the faint tinkle of music from an open porthole.

And as I sat there, pondering on my future, a line from Thoreau kept running through my head. 'Why should I feel lonely? Is not our planet in the Milky Way?'

Wherever I went, the stars were there to

keep me company. And I knew that as long as I responded, in both a physical and mystical way, to the natural world—sea, sun, earth, moon and stars—I would never feel lonely upon this planet.

Richard Jefferies

If I have enjoyed reading a book by a particular author, I will go out of my way to read that writer's other works, even if some of them have fallen into obscurity. Jefferies is still highly regarded, but some of his books were hard to find, and for several years *The Story of My Heart* was the only work of his that had come my way.

And I had read it several times.

There are some books which get better on the second or third reading, and this was one of them. The first reading was a hurried one. I was carried away by the writer's passion for nature and his descriptive powers. At the second reading I found deeper layers of meaning hidden beneath the prose that ran like a mountain stream. At the third reading I had entered the mind and heart of the writer; his very soul.

John Richard Jefferies was born in 1848, on a small farm in the south of England, and died thirty-nine years later, after a life of ill-health and great poverty. His books did not make much money, and he made a living from selling articles on country life to newspapers and magazines. Many of these nature writings were later collected and published as books.

It was while Jefferies was suffering from consumption that he wrote *The Story of My Heart* (1883). It is more than a nature book; it is a record of his spiritual development, a work of poetic and mystic vision. His contemporaries regarded him as an atheist, especially after the publication of *The Story of My Heart*. A solitary man, he wrote on the heightened consciousness that comes to consumptives; but although an invalid during his last years, he was at heart a lusty pagan, delighting in all physical emotion.

My copy of *The Story of My Heart* is the same one I picked up in England before returning to India over fifty years ago. It is now held together with the help of Sellotape and other adhesives. I treasure it not only for its text but also for the evocative wood engravings by Gertrude Hermes which were a feature of this particular edition.

Oddly enough, I discovered Richard Jefferies's two children's classics, *Wood Magic* (1881) and *Bevis: The Story of a Boy* (1882) only when I was in my sixties. *Wood Magic* is a mixture of realism and romance, in which talking animals play an important part—a device that was to be used later by Kipling in *The Jungle Book* series, and is now commonly used in many children's books.

Bevis, the boy, is at the centre of both books, and he is in fact Jefferies in his childhood persona, and reflects his complete empathy with nature:

As Bevis stood and looked down, the wind

161

caressed him and said, 'Goodbye, darling, I am going yonder, straight across to the blue valley and the blue sky, where they meet; but I shall be back again when you come next time. Now remember, my dear, to drink me—come up here and drink me.'

'I promise,' said Bevis. 'Goodbye, jolly old wind.'

Bevis gathered a wild harebell, and ran with the flower in his hand down the hill, and as he ran the wild thyme kissed his feet and said, 'Come again, Bevis, come again.'

From *The Story of My Heart* (1883)

by Richard Jefferies

Chapter 1

The story of my heart commences seventeen years ago. In the glow of youth there were times every now and then when I felt the necessity of a strong inspiration of soul-thought. My heart was dusty, parched for want of the rain of deep feeling; my mind arid and dry, for there is a dust which settles on the heart as well as that which falls on a ledge. It is injurious to the mind as well as to the body to be always in one place and always surrounded by the same circumstances. A species of thick clothing slowly grows about the mind, the pores are chocked, little habits become a part of existence, and by degrees the mind is enclosed in a husk. When this began to form I felt eager to escape from it, to throw it off like heavy clothing, to drink deeply once more at the fresh fountains of life. An inspiration—a long, deep breath of the pure air of thought—could alone give health to the heart.

There is a hill to which I used to resort at such periods. The labour of walking three miles to it, all the while gradually ascending, seemed to clear my blood of the heaviness accumulated at home. On a warm summer day the slow continued rise required continual effort, which carried away the sense of oppression. The familiar everyday scene was soon out of sight; I came to other trees, meadows and fields; I began to breathe a new air and to have a fresher aspiration. I restrained my soul till I reached the sward of the hill; psyche, the soul that longed to be loose. I would write psyche always instead of soul to avoid meanings which have become attached to the word soul, but it is awkward to do so. Clumsy indeed are all words the moment the wooden stage of commonplace life is left. I restrained psyche, my soul, till I reached and put my foot on the grass at the beginning of the green hill itself.

Moving up the sweet short turf, at every step my heart seemed to obtain a wider horizon of feeling; with every inhalation of rich, pure air, a deeper desire. The very light of the sun was whiter and more brilliant here. By the time I had reached the summit I had entirely forgotten the petty circumstances and the annoyances of existence. I felt myself, myself. There was an entrenchment on the summit, and going down into the fosse I walked round it slowly to recover breath. On the south-western side there was a spot where the outer bank had partially slipped, leaving a gap. There the view was over a broad plain, beautiful with wheat, and enclosed by a perfect amphitheatre of green hills. Through these hills there was no narrow groove, or pass, southwards, where the white clouds seemed to close in the horizon. Woods hid the scattered hamlets and farmhouses, so that I was quite alone.

I was utterly alone with the sun and the earth. Lying down on the grass, I spoke in my soul to the earth, the sun, the air, and the distant sea far beyond sight. I thought of the earth's firmness—I felt it bear me up; through the grassy couch there came an influence as if I could feel the great earth speaking to me. I thought of the wandering air—its pureness, which is its beauty; the air touched me and gave me something of itself. I spoke to the sea: though so far, in my mind I saw it, green at the rim of the earth and blue in deeper ocean; I desired to have its strength, its mystery and glory. Then I addressed the sun, desiring the soul equivalent of his light and brilliance, his endurance and unwearied race. I turned to the blue heaven over, gazing into its depth, inhaling its exquisite colour and sweetness. The rich blue of the unattainable flower of the sky drew my soul towards it, and there it rested, for pure colour is rest of heart. By all these I prayed; I felt an emotion of the soul beyond all definition; prayer is a puny thing to it, and the word is a rude sign to the feeling, but I know no other.

By the blue heaven, by the rolling sun bursting through untrodden space, a new ocean of ether every day unveiled. By the fresh and wandering air encompassing the world; by the sea sounding on the shore—the green sea white-flecked at the margin and the deep ocean; by the strong earth under me. Then, returning, I prayed by the sweet thyme, whose little flowers I touched with my hand; by the slender grass; by the crumble of dry chalky earth I took up and let fall through my fingers. Touching the crumble of earth, the blade of grass, the thyme flower, breathing the earth-encircling air, thinking of the sea and the sky, holding out my hand for the sunbeams to touch it, prone on the sward in token of deep reverence, thus I prayed that I might touch the unutterable existence infinitely higher than deity.

With all the intensity of feeling which exalted me, all the intense communion I held with the earth, the sun and sky, the stars hidden by the light, with the ocean—in no manner can the thrilling depth of these feelings be written—with these I prayed, as if they were the keys of an instrument, of an organ, with which I swelled forth the notes of my soul, redoubling my own voice by their power. The great sun burning with light; the strong earth, dear earth; the warm sky; the pure air; the thought of ocean; the inexpressible beauty of all filled me with a rapture, an ecstasy, an inflatus. With this inflatus, too, I prayed. Next to myself I came and recalled myself, my bodily existence. I held out my hand, the sunlight gleamed on the skin and the iridescent nails; I recalled the mystery and beauty of the flesh. I thought of the mind with which I could see the ocean sixty miles distant, and gather to myself its glory. I thought of my inner existence, that consciousness which is called the soul. These, that is, myself—I threw into the balance to weigh the prayer the heavier. My strength of body, mind and soul, I flung into it; I put forth my strength;

I wrestled and laboured, and toiled in might of prayer. The prayer, this soul-emotion was in itself— not for an object—it was a passion. I hid my face in the grass, I was wholly prostrated, I lost myself in the wrestle, I was rapt and carried away.

Becoming calmer, I returned to myself and thought, full of aspiration, steeped to the lips of my soul in desire. I did not then define, or analyse, or understand this. I see now that what I laboured for was soul-life, more soul-nature, to be exalted, to be full of soul-learning. Finally I rose, walked half a mile or so along the summit of the hill eastwards, to soothe myself and come to the common ways of life again. Had any shepherd accidentally seen me lying on the turf, he would only have thought that I was resting a few minutes; I made no outward show. Who could have imagined the whirlwind of passion that was going on within me as I reclined there! I was greatly exhausted when I reached home. Occasionally I went upon the hill deliberately, deeming it good to do so; then, again, this craving carried me away up there of itself. Though the principal feeling was the same, there were variations in the mode in which it affected me.

Sometimes on lying down on the sward I first looked up at the sky, gazing for a long time till I could see deep into the azure and my eyes were full of the colour; then I turned my face to the grass and thyme, placing my hands at each side of my face so as to shut out everything and hide myself. Having drunk deeply of the heaven above and felt the most glorious beauty of the day, and remembering the old, old sea, which (as it seemed to me) was but just yonder at the edge, I now became lost, and absorbed into the being or existence of the universe. I felt down deep into the earth under, and high above into the sky, and farther still to the sun and stars. Still farther beyond the stars into the hollow of space, and losing thus my separateness of being came to seem like a part of the whole. Then I whispered to the earth beneath, through the grass and rhyme, down into the depth of its ear, and again up to the starry space hid behind the blue of day. Travelling in an instant across the distant sea, I saw as if with actual vision the palms and coconut trees, the bamboos of India, and the cedars of the extreme south. Like a lake with islands the ocean lay before me, as clear and vivid as the plain beneath in a midst of the amphitheatre of hills.

With the glory of the great sea, I said, with the firm, solid and sustaining earth; the depth, distance, and expanse of ether; the age, tamelessness, and ceaseless motion of the ocean; the stars, and the unknown in space; by all those things which are most powerful known to me, and by those which exist, but of which I have no idea whatever, I pray. Further, by my own soul, that secret existence which above all other things bears the nearest resemblance to the ideal of spirit, infinitely nearer than earth, sun or star. Speaking by an inclination towards, not in words, my soul prays that I may have something from each of these, that I may gather a flower from them, that I may have in myself the secret and meaning of the earth, the golden sun, the light, the foam-flecked sea. Let my soul become enlarged; I am not enough; I am little and contemptible. I desire a greatness of soul, an irradiance of mind, a deeper insight, a broader hope. Give me power of soul, so that I may actually effect by its will that which I strive for.

In winter, though I could not then rest on the grass, or stay long enough to form any definite expression, I still went up to the hill once now and then, for it seemed that to merely visit the spot repeated all that I had previously said. But it was not only then.

In summer I went out into the fields, and let my soul inspire these thoughts under the trees, standing against the trunk, or looking up through the branches at the sky. If trees could speak, hundreds of them would say that I had had these soul-emotions under them. Leaning against the oak's massive trunk, and feeling the rough bark and the lichen at my back, looking southwards over the grassy fields, cowslip-yellow, at the woods on the slope, I thought of my desire of deeper soul-life. Or under the green firs, looking upwards, the sky was more deeply blue at their tops; then the brake fern was unrolling, the doves cooing, the thickets astir, the late ash leaves coming forth. Under the shapely rounded elms, by the hawthorn bushes and hazel, everywhere the same deep desire for the soul-nature; to have from all green things and from the sunlight the inner meaning which was not known to them, that I might be full of light as the woods of the sun's rays. Just to touch the lichened bark of a tree, or the end of a spray projecting over the path as I walked, seemed to repeat the same prayer in me.

The long-lived summer days dried and warmed the turf in the meadows. I used to lie down in solitary corners at full length on my back, so as to feel the embrace of the earth. The grass stood high above me, and the shadows of the tree branches danced on my face. I looked up at the sky, with half-closed eyes to bear the dazzling light. Bees buzzed over me, sometimes a butterfly passed, there was a hum in the air, greenfinches sang in the hedge. Gradually entering into the intense life of the summer days—a life which burned around as if every grass blade and leaf were a torch—I came to feel the long-drawn life of the earth back into the dimmest past, while the sun of the moment was warm on me. Sesostris on the most ancient sands of the south, in ancient, ancient days, was conscious of himself and of the sun. This sunlight linked me through the ages to that past consciousness. From all the ages my soul desired to take that soul-life which had flowed through them as the sunbeams had continually poured on earth. As the hot sands take up the heat, so would I take up that soul-energy. Dreamy in appearance, I was breathing full of existence; I was aware of the grass blades, the flowers, the leaves on hawthorn and tree. I seemed to live more largely through them, as if each were a pore through which I drank. The grasshoppers called and leaped, the greenfinches sang, the blackbirds happily fluted, all the air hummed with life. I was plunged deep in existence, and with all that existence I prayed.

Through every grass blade in the thousand, thousand grasses; through the million leaves, veined and edge-cut, on bush and tree; through the song notes and the marked feathers of the birds; through the insects' hum and the colour of the butterflies; through the soft, warm air, the flecks of clouds dissolving—I used them all for prayer. With all the energy the sunbeams had poured unwearied on the earth since Sesostris was conscious of them on the ancient sands; with all the life that had been lived by vigorous man and beauteous woman since first in dearest Greece the dream of the gods was woven; with all the soul-life that had flowed a long stream down to me, I prayed that I might have a soul more than equal to, far beyond my conception of, these things of the past, the present, and the fullness of all life. Not only equal to these, but beyond, higher, and more powerful than I could imagine. That I might take from all their energy, grandeur and beauty, and gather it into me. That my soul might be more than the cosmos of life.

I prayed with the glowing clouds of sunset and the soft light of the first star coming through the violet sky. At night with the stars, according to the season: now with the Pleiades, now with the Swan or burning Sirius, and broad Orion's whole constellation, red Aldebaran, Arcturus, and the Northern Crown; with the morning star, the light-bringer, once now and then when I saw it, a white-gold ball in the violet-purple sky, or framed about with pale summer vapour floating away as red streaks shot horizontally in the east. A diffused saffron ascended into the luminous upper azure. The disk of the sun rose over the hill, fluctuating with throbs of light; his chest heaved in fervour of brilliance. All the glory of the sunrise filled me with broader and furnace-like vehemence of prayer. That I might have the deepest of soul-life, the deepest of all, deeper far than all this greatness of the visible universe and even of the invisible; that I might have a fullness of soul till now unknown, and utterly beyond my own conception.

In the deepest darkness of the night the same thought rose in my mind as in the bright light of noontide. What is there which I have not used to strengthen the same emotion?

Favourite Books
by Favourite Authors

Charles Dickens	David Copperfield; Nicholas Nickleby; Barnaby Rudge; The Pickwick Papers; Our Mutual Friend; Oliver Twist; Sketches by Boz
Emily Brontë	Wuthering Heights; Poems
Honoré de Balzac	Eugénie Grandet; Le Père Goriot
André Gide	The Immoralist; The Fruits of the Earth; Journals
W. Somerset Maugham	Cakes and Ale; The Moon and Sixpence; Collected Stories; The Summing Up; A Writer's Notebook

Joseph Conrad	Typhoon; Youth; The Shadow-Line; An Outcast of the Islands; Heart of Darkness; Tales of Unrest
Hugh Walpole	Fortitude; Mr Perrin and Mr Traill; The Cathedral; All Souls' Night; Portrait of a Man with Red Hair
William Saroyan	My Name Is Aram; The Bicycle Rider in Beverly Hills; The Human Comedy
Evelyn Waugh	Decline and Fall; Put Out More Flags; Scoop; Vile Bodies
R.L. Stevenson	Treasure Island; The Ebb-Tide; Travels with a Donkey in the Cévennes; 'The Beach of Falesá' (South Sea Tales); A Child's Garden of Verses; Dr Jekyll and Mr Hyde

H.E. Bates	My Uncle Silas; Seven Tales and Alexander; Country Tales
Raymond Chandler	The Big Sleep; The High Window; Farewell, My Lovely; The Lady in the Lake
J.M. Barrie	Dear Brutus; Mary Rose; A Kiss for Cinderella; Peter Pan; Quality Street; Shall We Join the Ladies?
J.B. Priestley	The Good Companions; Angel Pavement; They Walk in the City; Bright Day; Lost Empires
M.R. James	Ghost Stories of an Antiquary; A Warning to the Curious and Other Ghost Stories